HANNAH FREE

Claudia Allen

Bella
BOOKS
2010

Bella Books, Inc.
P.O. Box 10543
Tallahassee, FL 32302

Printed in the United States of America on acid-free paper
First Edition

Editor: Karin Kallmaker
Cover Designer: Linda Callaghan

ISBN 13:978-1-59493-172-7

Also by Claudia Allen

Acknowledgments

Hannah Free has had an unusual evolution from play to film and now into this novel.

The story of *Hannah Free* was written to put a human face on lesbian legal rights. I also wanted to tell a complicated, cradle to grave, warts and all, great lesbian love story. It's a work of imagination about all the real Hannahs and Rachels who never had their stories told.

So *Hannah Free* first came to life as a play in a premiere at Bailiwick Rep in Chicago. L.M. Attea was the director. David Zak was artistic director. This play has had many productions from Miami to Madison to Arkansas, and I thank all of the theater artists who have brought Hannah to life and kept her on the road.

So many people put their hearts and talents and savings into making *Hannah Free* a film and I thank them all. Special thanks to Wendy Jo Carlton for her direction and her dedication to filmmaking. The cast is a family album of some of my favorite Chicago actors, so thank you Meg, Maureen, Elaine, Les, Kelli, Ann, Jacqui, Kate, Brad, Jeanne, Sarah, Pat, Taylor and all the rest for giving the characters in this work their full humanity. Thank you, investors, donors and our producer Tracy Baim and her sainted family. Tracy made this happen.

And, of course, I can never thank Sharon Gless enough for being Hannah. Sharon is the best as a friend and as an actor. Her skill in front of a camera, her passion, her commitment, her bravery, her humor, and her loving heart

were such a gift to this film and to all of us involved and all who see it.

And now *Hannah Free*: the novel. Thank you to my hardworking editor Karin Kallmaker for all her enthusiasm and insights, and my publisher Linda Hill of Bella Books for suggesting I write this novel and promising to publish it if I did. And she did. And Linda and Karin respected my desire to let this novel have its own life, its own fresh take on this story and not just be a simplistic novel. I enjoyed being given the chance to learn more of Hannah and Rachel's story than we could fit into a film with a very tight budget.

Personal thanks to my sister Suzy and her husband Jim and to my dad, Duane, and my late great mom, Cleo, and to all my friends (Bruce, Carrie, Mike, Randy, Jeanne, Carol, Theresa, Bob, Toni and Toni and so many others), my exes (especially Cathy and Jorjet), and my cats.

Claudia Allen, January, 2010

About the Author

Claudia Allen grew up in Clare, Michigan, graduated from the University of Michigan, taught at the University of Chicago, and has been an acclaimed Chicago playwright for many years. A resident playwright at Chicago's Tony-winning Victory Gardens Theater, Claudia has had the honor of working with many terrific Chicago actors, her great director and friend Sandy Shinner, and legends Julie Harris and Sharon Gless. *Hannah Free* is Claudia's first film and her first novel.

Dedicated to my dear friend, my Hannah Free,
SHARON GLESS

Chapter One

HANNAH

My name is Hannah Free and this is the story of my lifelong love affair with the sweetest, most stubborn woman in the world.

Rachel and I met when she was six and I was seven. I first caught sight of her at a Fourth of July parade in town, but we weren't properly introduced until her first day of school in the fall. We were both farm girls but lived a couple of miles apart, and I was no churchgoer, so school was our first real opportunity to meet. I'd barely made it into second grade as she was starting first.

My first year at that one-room Klee School was society's first attempt to tame me, and it hadn't gone well. Miss Myrtle Duffield laid the ruler on my knuckles on a regular basis. And I just as regularly disappeared out the back window and into the woods. But ruler or no ruler, despite grammar and

the multiplication tables and having to read about Grover Cleveland, once I saw Rachel, age six, sitting two rows over, hair tied up in a pink ribbon, my attendance at the Klee School improved dramatically. And the first time she smiled at me, my goose was cooked.

Let me pause here and give you the lay of the land. I don't have it in me to write a straightforward narrative like you're probably used to reading. All my life I've followed the wind and my thumb wherever they'll take me—Paris, New Mexico, South America, Alaska—so this book's gonna have to follow my life tangents. But it will also have to follow me back to Rachel, because that's where every road and railroad car, boat and airplane ever took me—home to Rachel.

That's where I am now, in this gloomy old mansion of a town nursing home in 1991, an ornery old coot who fell off the roof shoveling snow and didn't heal up so good. Rachel's up here too, laid low by old age, a stroke and a coma, but she's off in another wing. And they won't let me see her.

"They" is Rachel's daughter, Marge. I helped raise her, part of the way anyway, but she don't approve of her mother and me—and she's heard enough bed noises over the years to know what that means, what we were—are—to each other. Marge liked me when she was little, but she's been a royal pain in the ass ever since she joined the Baptist Church. And as Rachel's daughter she's her legal family so she's got the legal right to keep us apart. And I've got no legal rights, none, to see the woman I've loved all my life.

"Hannah, time for your juice."

The nurses up here are always after me with something, pokin' and proddin' me and handing me little cups with pills or juice or milk. Why can't they leave me the hell alone?

I pipe up and tell her, "Don'tcha know I'm allergic to orange juice?"

This sturdy soul is pleasant to me but treats me like I'm a not-so-bright three-year-old. "Is that on your chart, Hannah?"

"It oughta be." I plant my arms across my chest and stick out my bottom lip. (If my mama was alive, she'd warn me to watch out or a bird might perch on it.)

"Hannah, are you sure you're allergic to orange juice?"

Okay, the truth of it is I'm just sick of it. Get to be my age there are just things you're sick and tired of like orange juice and country music and *Wheel of Fortune*.

This nurse, this Cleo, goes off to her cart to get me some milk instead. She's got the goddamnedest plastic turquoise earrings on. I bet she's a real cutup at the bowling alley. Hell, she could be one of the girls, if you know what I mean, but up here to the Home all I get to see is her nurse face.

When she comes back with my milk and a pill, I ask her if I can see Rachel; tell her I need to see Rachel; we need to see each other. This is no way for us to end our days, together but apart.

"Now watch your blood pressure, Hannah."

I guess I got kinda loud. And red. But I *need* to see Rachel, like a horse needs water.

Cleo don't know what to make of me—people in this town never did—but she tries to jolly me along, humor me until her shift is over and she gets to go home to a nice cold six-pack in her trailer over by Lake Thirteen. "She's an old friend is she, Rachel?"

"Friend don't begin to say it. Please we need to see each other. I don't want Rachel to be alone."

"But she's not alone, honey. Her daughter sits with her for hours and hours every day."

Lucky her. Why can't I?

"It's sweet to see how devoted Marge is to her mother. So many people up here don't get any visitors."

Like me.

Cleo fluffs my pillow and tries to make her getaway, but I grab her hand. "Please! Please let me see Rachel!"

"You just drink the rest of your milk and then we'll see." She gently but firmly pries her hand loose.

3

"Wait." I'm so desperate, I gulp down the milk like a kid eager to please. Eighty years old and I'm brought to this. But I don't care. I'll do anything to win this woman over, anything to see Rachel.

"Good girl."

Good *girl*, like I'm in kindergarten. Jesus Christ.

"It would mean a lot to both of us." But I keep trying. I don't have any allies in this place and I need one bad. I treat Cleo to a warm, wistful look—or try to. I'm not good at warm and even worse at wistful. I probably just look bound up.

"Well, we want what's best for both of you. That's what we're here for." And off she goes.

Who can blame her? You never woulda caught me washing old people's butts when I was her age. And before she knows it she'll be in one of these beds herself sucking oxygen through a tube. It's no way to live. Cleo oughta get herself a job outside in the fresh air.

That's what I always tried to do. I was kind of a jackass of all trades. I flew planes, detailed boats, bought and sold cattle, anything to make a buck. I even taught school (my one indoor job) in Barrow, Alaska—I bet Miss Myrtle Duffield would roll over in her grave if she knew that.

I learned how to do most of the outdoorsy stuff plus fix cars from my older brothers and my Uncle Mack. It was obvious early on that Mama didn't have a daughter to raise, not a gingham-dress-learn-to-embroider kinda daughter anyway, so she turned me over to the men. Uncle Mack was really my stepdaddy—he stepped in for Daddy who took off for World War I and never came back. He didn't die—he just never came back.

Rachel's family was more traditional, but less loving. Her family practically needed a second vehicle just to tote all their Bibles to church. Her ma was a stern, tart-tongued creature who did teach Rachel to cook the best fried chicken in the county. It's too bad that ornery old Dutch woman only got

4

to run the house and not the farm. Rachel's pompous little pa was no great shakes as a farmer, always planting too late or the wrong thing. So the whole bunch of 'em were eager for Rachel to marry well and bring some prosperity to the family. Before she'd hardly even sprouted breasts they were inviting boys to come porchsit with her.

And Rachel tried to be a good daughter, she really did. She'd sit there on the porch bored out of her skull listening to some thick-lipped oaf rattle on about the baseball game he starred in or how many acres his pa planned to plant to wheat, and Rachel would rock and nod and look off into her thoughts of me.

We were just naturally drawn to each other the way people are. She thought I was funny and, oh, I tried to be when she was looking, practically broke my neck trying to make her laugh or just smile my way.

When we were little girls, me in my boys' overalls, Rachel in her home-sewn dresses, I'd chase her through the corn with a frog or a dead snake. Or I'd find a pretty stone or a fossil, anything to get her attention so I could just look at her while she examined the puddin' stone or gave the snake a burial under her pear tree.

At first, I admit I was mostly just drawn—stupefied really—by her beauty, for Rachel was always a beauty. Perfect features. Neat as a pin. Long brown hair, always long even after she was an old lady, long flowing hair to lose my hands in.

But as the years, decades went by it was everything else about Rachel that made me stay in love.

She was fair, considerate, nurturing and funnier than people realized. Pretty as she was, she was never vain, never judged other people on their looks or lack of teeth. A tireless worker, Rachel kept a house that was spotless but comfortable, homey you might say.

She made a beef roast that melted in your mouth. She knitted lap robes for the invalids and took them her homemade

chicken noodle soup. She baked bread that made her house smell like heaven.

Then when I showed up with a bucket of sunfish, she'd fry them up for my supper, even if it stunk up her house for days.

Rachel had her temper and her stubbornness. She could get furious, but eventually forgive. She was too gentle and kindhearted not to forgive.

What I probably loved most of all about her was Rachel was just so kind, kind to me, kind to everybody. She took in stray people for Thanksgiving and Christmas and always took the underdog's side in local gossip. She was my greatest defender. Much as I loved her body, what really hooked me was how sensitive she was, how protective of people's feelings. She was a good, kindhearted person through and through.

Of course, that used to get me in trouble.

One day at recess at the Klee School, I made fun of one of the little girls who didn't get picked to play the games because she was kinda plump and got winded. I called that poor sweet little girl Porky and made her cry. Rachel heard and slugged me so hard in the arm I almost started to cry myself.

"Why would you do that? Be mean to Karen Schneider when she's never done a thing to you?" Rachel was right up in my face in that dirt playground with its one swing dangling from a tree, and her fists were still clenched, ready to let me have it again. I knew she was upset and I was supposed to be feeling scared or contrite, but instead I was basking in her attention like she'd just told me I was a genius.

Rachel could tell her words weren't having the effect she wanted so she slugged me again and poked her cute little finger in my face. "You be nice to Karen, Hannah, or I'll never speak to you again."

I felt like I'd been kicked right in the chest by our old milk cow Bessie. I could barely breathe. "I'm sorry." This time I meant it.

Rachel looked me up and down like a seven-year-old middle-aged woman. "Fine. Now go tell her that."

We locked eyes. Held the gaze way longer than we strictly needed to. Then I nodded and, rubbing my arm for theatrical effect, I trudged off to tell Karen Schneider how sorry I was and how bad I felt for hurting her feelings and did she want some of my licorice? Rachel watched the apology from across the playground and nodded with satisfaction when she saw Karen accept one of my treasured black licorice whips from the general store in town. Smiling over at Rachel, I offered Karen a second whip and unfortunately she accepted.

I could see Rachel chuckle at my expense before she turned away to jump rope—I couldn't actually hear the laugh but I could see it in her eyes.

Feeling as high as a kite, I told Karen Schneider that tomorrow she should be on my team at dodgeball and damned if she wasn't good at it. That big girl could throw a mean dodgeball, usually at some boy's head. Karen and me always got along after that. And she always stayed friendly with Rachel over the years even when other women in the town looked at her funny because of me.

Lying in my bed up to the Home with my eyes closed, I replay this whole playground scene with Rachel and Karen and my licorice whips like it's a summer rerun on the TV. Can you blame me that I'd rather tune in and see what's playing in my memory rather than open my eyes and look at what sadness is playing up here to the nursing home? Old coots wander past my doorway lost, pants full of poop, looking for their mama who's been dead since the 1918 flu.

One old lady always rolls by in her wheelchair clutching her dolly. In fact, there she is now just as Rachel's daughter Marge is sliming her way down the hall to my doorway. Marge is a genius at putting her foot in her mouth. Never fails. I see her lean over the old lady with the dolly and ask how her baby is today. And that old lady swings her head around and gives Marge just the most clear-eyed, scathing look and roars, "It's a doll!"

7

Now some scenes are worth watching out my doorway. Marge backs away from that wheelchair like she's been bit by a rattlesnake and clutches her purse tighter to her chest—I guess she's got Fort Knox in there because she never sets that purse down.

Marge steps into my room, wound up tight with her tightly permed church lady hair and her blouse and sweater buttoned up so high breathing must be a chore. "Hello, Hannah."

I forget to say hello to the old battle-ax, because I'm enjoying a brief flashback of Rachel making a meatloaf. I loved watching that woman cook. Loved watching her strong hands work that meat.

Marge clears her throat and puts on her talking-to-deaf old-people voice. "HELLO, HANNAH."

I jump. "Jesus, Marge. I can hear. Just can't walk worth a shit. And sorry, toots, but I'm not dead either so dial it down."

We glower at each other, a stare down kinda like two gunfighters in the middle of the street on *Gunsmoke*. Then she takes a couple steps further into the room, inching her way in like she's avoiding quicksand. Marge frowns at a photo of me and Rachel on my dresser, then squints over at the postcards I've got tacked up on a board on the wall like she's expecting to see porno. Even my plants and the sunshine streaming in the window seem to annoy her.

"I hear you've been wanting to see Mom." Man, she's got a prissy prune-faced look on her. I wish I did have a six-shooter under the Indian blanket on my bed—lucky I don't.

"Of course, I want to see your mother, Marge. It's not right you keeping us apart like this." We lock eyes again, pure anger.

"I can't have you upsetting her."

"Upset!" Steam's coming out my ears. I'm seeing red. "When have I ever upset your mother?"

"All her life." Marge is pissed and a pisshead, but she's sincere, you gotta give her that. She dearly loves Rachel and

she's honestly furious with me because I caused her mother a lotta grief—it's a pity she's forgotten all the joy.

"Please, Marge, please let me see her. You know this isn't right." I try to look pitiful, but I'm afraid I'm about as cuddly as a bull in heat.

"Mom needs peace. You never brought her peace."

"She brought me something better." Okay, so it's not Rachel in the flesh who's in my room defending me. And no one can hear her but me, not even her own daughter. But she's here, standing right over there in the light. Rachel, the physical Rachel, may be trapped in that coma, but some days when I get lucky, her spirit comes to visit me. And it's quite a sight to see, her looking thirty-two again, long chestnut hair, dancing eyes, wearing her apron and a sweater pushed up to her elbows, looking like she's just about ready to bake some pies.

She watches Marge shoot me one more dirty look from the doorway. "I'll tell Mama you asked after her. She won't hear, but I'll tell her. Goodbye, Hannah."

Good riddance. Rachel and me watch Marge flounce out the door, back ramrod stiff.

"She used to be such a cute little girl." I say this to Rachel's spirit, who looks like I remember her on that Sunday in December '41, when we sat and listened to the radio all day, to the news about Pearl Harbor. Rachel has that same concerned look in her eye. But then she shrugs it off, smiles and moves closer to the bed. I sure wish I could touch her, but that's not how this spirit business works.

Rachel smiles tenderly. "Marge was always jealous of you."

I find myself just looking at her, memorizing every detail, forgetting to talk—which is something for me.

"Hello?! Are you Grandma Hannah? Hello..."

"Goddammit." Somebody else is interrupting us, a cute young thing at least, dark hair in her eyes, petite, possibly jailbait, cute. I remember just in time I'm pissed.

"Who the hell are you? What do you want?"

"They told me—"

"They who?" I bellow, really laying it on. I'm enjoying myself.

The kid, backpack slung over her shoulder, tries to stand her ground. "I'm writing my senior thesis on women's herstory, and the nurse at the desk said to ask Grandma Hannah—"

"Jesus Christ, stop calling me that!"

The kid jumps back a foot and hides behind her hair. "Sorry."

I'm feeling just a teensy bit sorry for her, but I'm giving this performance to amuse Rachel even if she isn't really here. And she is smiling, so it's worth it. "Well what? The Depression? Women's suffrage? The Civil War? Whad'ya need my sage words about? I'm busy."

College girl gives me a little smile frown through her bangs. Cute. "The Depression."

She pulls off her sweatshirt. It's always hot in this damn place. Then she makes herself at home in the standard issue visitors chair, pulling a notepad and pen out of her knapsack.

An audience. I may look all red and belligerent but I'm in my element, happy as a clam. A cute little chickie's undivided attention? I feel like I'm twenty again. "I went to Alaska. Caught everything I ate except chocolate. Didn't need much money so I mailed most of my pay home to a lady friend with kids. War came, I lied about my age—I was afraid I was too old. Thought the WACS might want somebody with a few less miles on them. But I could fly so I looked pretty good to them. Spent the war flying cargo in and out of New Mexico. Afterward, I wondered what was in those planes."

She's scribbling away, captivated to be sitting right next to a big lump of living history like myself.

"The Fifties I bought and sold cattle in Brazil, worked the docks, worked overseeing the baggers at the Pioneer Sugar plant and invested in computer stocks which is how come a Depression rat like me can afford this beauteous suite in Hotel

Hell. I voted for Roosevelt because I liked Eleanor. That's it. Posterity." I nonchalantly adjust the sheet on my hospital bed and glance over to see if she's bored or still captivated.

The kid gives me a shy, cute look through her hair as she adjusts her sock, still captivated. "I guess you get asked this a lot."

"No shit." I ruffle up my tail feathers like an old rooster. "I'm the only coherent old fart in this place. They send you in here like you'll perk me up. What am I? The public library? Go ask your parents what it was like growing up in the Sixties."

Now that gets her. Her pretty brown Natalie Wood eyes flash and her head jerks up like a riled up pony. "My parents are dead."

"Well, so are mine."

She glares. I fume. Gritting our teeth, we stare each other down for about ten seconds, then we both burst out laughing. We're enjoying each other and it's our way of finally admitting it.

As we start to quiet down and wipe away a stray tear from all that laughing, an old woman wanders by calling for her granny. I'm a tough old bird, but that's hard to watch, especially how desperate she is. The nurses have to tell that old lady over and over, day after day that her granny is dead and buried over in the Catholic cemetery. But she forgets by the next day, next hour, and goes on looking for her.

Cutie-pie gives me a sad look. "What an awful place."

No argument here. "Always keep a gun handy in case you bust yourself up so bad you need to put yourself out of your misery. Now up in Alaska if I fell off a roof a bear woulda ate me, got some good outa me."

"You've really been to Alaska?" The girl scoots her chair closer—I've still got it. Out of the corner of my eye, I can see shadow Rachel shaking her head. I've always been a first-class flirt. Nice that Rachel can still be jealous of an old wreck like me.

"I lived in Alaska."

11

Rachel snorts. "Robbing the cradle."

"Nonsense." I snort right back at her.

Poor confused kid can't see Rachel, who's not really there even if I do see her. "Living in Alaska's nonsense?"

My eyes dart over to Rachel—always my favorite place to look—and I try to cover. "I'm just mumbling to myself. Us old people do that. Nah, Alaska was swell. I was real happy living up there."

That was a low blow. Rachel lowers her eyebrows, pouts her lips and gives me that disgusted look again. If Rachel wasn't a lady, she'd give me the finger.

Alaska. Three long years away from each other. Our first really long time apart after growing up together and fingering each other in half the haymows in the county. Okay, that's an exaggeration, but you get my drift.

The kid leans forward, all ears. "How did you survive in Alaska?"

"I had my high school diploma, so I taught school, skinned things. You get by."

Now that was a funny line, but this kid is too earnest to laugh at it. "I admire you, Hannah. You just went and did it. Most people dream and stay home."

Rachel shoots me a pouty look. "There's nothing wrong with staying home."

The kid is blushing—so earnest. "I'd really love to go to Africa, but I'm afraid I might need a blood transfusion."

"Are you sick?"

"No."

"Then don't get sick."

"The blood supply in Africa is so tainted with AIDS, what if something did happen?"

"God forbid something should happen in your life!" I'm bellowing again, but we're both enjoying it.

"Wow, that's a great philosophy." Kiddo beams at me.

I bask and enjoy the view. About Rachel's height, shoulder-length brown hair, no bra under that vintage Bette Midler T-

shirt. I always did enjoy new scenery.

Rachel scowls. "I really don't care to watch this."

I scowl right back. "You call this something? I went to your wedding."

We'd kissed as children (a lot), but the first time I ever had her was that summer. I milked my widowed Aunt Hazel's six Herefords while Rachel watched and stroked their noses. I'd squirt that warm milk in Rachel's mouth like she was a kitten, and she'd lean down and let me kiss her milky mouth. Eventually I was squirting milk down her camisole and one thing led to another.

I pulled her down into a horse stall and with shaky hands got her dress unbuttoned. She pulled me up to kiss her some more, but then she didn't object when I buried my face in her chest and started to suck the cows' milk off her breasts. Her nipples were hard in my mouth so I kept licking and sucking them long after the milk was digested. Rachel moaned when I sucked harder, taking her whole breast in my mouth, so my fingers just kind of naturally found their way up under her skirt and petticoat and dug away at her underdrawers until I was sliding a finger up into her, taking her virginity, a bloodless taking but I knew I was the first ever allowed in there.

Rachel's chestnut brown hair flooded down her back as she arched against my hand, and I kissed her throat and her ears and deep in her mouth until she finally made a strangled noise and fell upward against me.

And eventually I carried the pails of milk into the house for Aunt Hazel to churn, and Rachel walked home across the fields and sat on her parents' porch with Mr. Johnson and smiled pleasantly while he fumbled for conversation and she tightened her legs together under her dress, still feeling me. I imagine her breath getting shallower while Mr. Johnson rambled on, oblivious. At least, I like to think that's how her evening went. By then I was in town with my brothers, sipping moonshine and playing poker with the preacher's son in the coal room in the basement of the Baptist Church, trying not to think about Mr. Johnson holding my girl's hand.

But as the summer wore on, Mr. Johnson inched closer on the swing and probably started stealing kisses, and Rachel's father, full of the wrath of God, grew more belligerent to live

with. Finally, despite more couplings with me in the barn, despite her climbing on top of me the day after I'd taken her and letting me have it, her strong hands kneading me like bread dough, despite all that, Rachel said "I do" to Mr. Johnson, the dullest man she could find, and marched down the aisle with him in August.

And I watched. Actually she didn't march, she just stood next to her parents' Macintosh apple tree and said she'd be Mr. Johnson's wife to have and to hold from this day forward. I stood beside my brother Dave, who suspected what Rachel was to me but had no words for it. We grimly watched Mr. Johnson kiss the bride, and we choked down a slice of yellow wedding cake with white frosting. And that night, I hopped a freight and took off for Alaska so I wouldn't have to watch Rachel be Mrs. Johnson.

She was mystified and furious about me leaving, but I didn't see how I had a choice. I couldn't just be Rachel's friend. So I went as far away as I could to a place where I'd have to concentrate so hard on not freezing to death maybe I could get through a minute or two without thinking of her.

My mind quite willingly starts to slip out of this painful moment in our past and back into that nursing home hospital bed, back to give the kid my full attention. She's beaming at me expectantly. I take one more look at Rachel's face in the barn that first time she came, then I slide back into the present.

Oops. I give the kid a sage look then slip back into my memory for one more flashback, to Alaska and a confession. Alaska was my first experience of both avalanches and other women. If Rachel was going to give herself to someone else, even if it was the languid and inept Mr. Johnson, I was going to bed other women, possibly even in a real bed. I wish I could tell you I was faithful to Rachel with my body, but I wasn't— my heart was faithful, still is, but my body wandered.

In Alaska, it was sometimes simply a matter of warmth.

17

I specialized in the big gals in Alaska, because they kept me thawed. Right after I arrived, I met a hefty Eskimo gal named Daisy who pumped gas, and I'll not refrain from saying we pumped each other. She did keep me warm through that long first winter. Daisy also taught me to fly. The first time she took me up, we flew past Mount Denali and landed on a frozen river. Startled a moose. The she handed me the controls and started drinking Jim Beam from a flask while I tried not to kill us getting that plane back up in the sky. Great gal, that Daisy, multitalented, but we were both just too butch to last. It was practically big-time wrestling every night over who got to be on top. For some reason, love, trust, I could let Rachel take me sometimes, be vulnerable, but most times I liked to be in control—so did Daisy. Oh well. Bless her heart, she did teach me how to fly.

There were others, including a wiry gal, Nettie Bobo, who lived near the salmon and still drops me a postcard when she visits her sister in Homer. Like me and Daisy, Nettie preferred her women femme, but population is sparse in Alaska, and us dykes tended to cozy up when we'd stumble onto each other— it wouldn't last, but it made things less lonely, less empty for a month or two.

Teaching school, I also sampled my share of married mothers whose husbands would go off on seal hunts for weeks at a time. The ladies'd stop by my room to ask how their daughters and sons were doing in school, and pretty soon they'd be giving me the eye, and unless I had a cold I was happy to burrow under their fur coats and oblige 'em. I'd make them happy for a night or two, but I put up some pretty high walls around my igloo, willing to touch but not be touched.

All these arctic encounters helped me know I wasn't the only woman who wanted to be with women "that way." So they were good for me, but didn't mean much. I'd given one woman power over me—never again. So after a night or two of making my bedsprings groan, I'd send these women home

to wait for their husbands to bring home the blubber. There was only one married woman I really wanted, and it was killing me not to have her.

And as much as I lusted for Rachel, buying Lux soap because it smelled like her, what I really missed most was talking with her. I didn't have very many long conversations in Alaska. I'd talk trapping and fishing with the men over whiskey we'd fly in from Canada to sidestep Prohibition. And I'd help kids and sometimes their parents learn to read. But I kept my soul to myself.

What idiot loses her soul to another person at seven? And again and again until she's barely nineteen and the other person marries someone else?

I could tell Rachel anything and better yet she told me things I know she never breathed to another human being. We had thoughts and conversations women weren't supposed to have, at least not in 1930. Where we came from, you weren't supposed to question the inherent rightness of so many things that were so wrong. Men ruling the roost, Jim Crow racism, the sanctity of Calvin Coolidge. And the God's truth that Jesus was a Republican and trade unions came straight from the devil. Rachel didn't question the way things were as often as I did, but she let me say my piece, and then she'd nod and make a point that would blow my tirade out of the water.

We could talk and listen for hours, sprawled under my grandma's maple on the north hill above Grandma's bean fields, watching the squirrels chase each other through the branches of that sugar maple. We'd look around, kiss quickly, then talk some more until the pink streamers of sunset sent us home.

We had such amazing conversations all our lives, whether we were twelve or seventy, and I missed that with a physical mourning after she married Mr. Johnson and I left for Alaska. Maybe some of these other women could hold a conversation through the long night of those Alaskan winters, but I was afraid to risk finding out, afraid to risk losing another Rachel.

Not that there was one.

All those three years in Alaska, I always thought of Rachel. I'd close my eyes and there she'd be, leaning on her elbow under that maple or picking straw out of my hair in the barn. I sent her a note and money every so often—I didn't trust any man to give Rachel everything she needed. And I needed to write her, even just to send twenty dollars and a scribbled note about watching a hawk circling overhead. I'd been connected to Rachel all my life; I needed to stay connected somehow, to keep up the conversation if only one-sided on paper.

And I wrote her bad poetry I never sent and I started writing journals where I'd mix talk of the day's fishing with a description of the color of Rachel's pussy and how it tasted, and I wrote how unlikely it was I'd ever be a published writer, my dream, writing about the taste of pussy.

The kid is looking at me kind of funny. "You went to whose wedding?" (Which is the last thing she heard.)

I wave off the question, a little testy—I'm not going to that damn wedding in my memory again. Besides, I'm kind of embarrassed. I probably seem as senile as the rest of these old bats walking the halls with their dollies. "Never mind. Forget it." But I do look over at spirit Rachel who shakes her head at me then moves closer to the window to watch a freight train rumble by. Her profile, kind of like that eagle, makes me breathless for a moment, but then I drag myself back into the encounter that's really happening. "So kid, you married?"

She shakes her head and smiles, amused. "Nope."

I look back over at Rachel's spirit who's now watching a deer loping away from the freight. I go ahead and talk to Rachel even if it does seem weird to the kid. "Hard to tell these days. Girls who were that way used to wear a pinkie ring, men's socks." I look at the girl. "How old are you?"

"Twenty-one." She's proud to say it, legal, no stranger to a few beers. I look her over again, the no makeup, the rumpled T-shirt, the no bra. Well, maybe she don't know yet, but I

sure did and long before I was twenty-one. "Were you ever married, Hannah?"

"Not to a man."

Her eyes are sparkling. "Oh yeah?" I made her day. We make the kind of eye contact I would have followed up on if I was forty years younger. "This gonna go in your paper?"

"Maybe. Is she dead?"

"Almost." I look over at Rachel's spirit standing near the window. "She's up here, too, over in that other wing, but they won't let me see her. She's in a coma, but they still won't let me see her. They're 'protecting' us from each other. People were always doing that."

"That's awful." She looks pissed off on my behalf, then she suddenly gets an *aha* look on her face. She's just figured something else out. "Is she who you talk to?"

Pretty smart. "Since they won't let me go to her, I bring her to me—or she comes on her own. I'm not really sure how it works, but she comes to visit me—her spirit comes—so we get to talk."

"I still talk to my parents, especially Mom, especially at night when I can't sleep."

After she says it, she looks embarrassed, self-conscious like only the young can look, so afraid of saying something stupid, of being laughed at—not me. I've been putting my foot in my mouth my whole life. It belongs there; fits like a glove.

"Kid, it's not like I'm gonna tell anybody. And Rachel won't tell, will ya, Rachel?" Rachel smiles, shakes her head. "So you're pretty damn safe telling me anything." So spill, will ya, kid? It's not often I get to play Spot The Dyke up to the nursing home.

But she's not a mind reader and her mind's on her parents. "They died about a year ago. Car accident."

"Rachel had her stroke about then. I woulda taken care of her at home if I hadn't been laid up in here myself—busted myself up good falling off that roof. Shoulda just let that snow

melt—or cave in the roof—but I always tried to keep Rachel's roof clear and her grass mowed."

"Rachel, huh? Pretty name."

"Pretty lady." I look over at Rachel. "Her family's got all the legal rights, that damn holier-than-thou daughter of hers, so here I sit." I clench my fists and shift around on the bed, ready to have a stroke myself thinking about it.

"So Rachel's just over in the other wing?"

"Beats me all to hell what they think I'm gonna do to her. I just wanna say goodbye." Dammit, I'm not gonna cry. But I can feel my eyes stinging. Goddamn Marge. I blink hard a couple of times.

The kid's watching me like a hawk. So is Rachel. "Hannah, that doesn't seem like too much to ask, just to see her, to see Rachel."

"It's like I lost all my goddamn rights." I grit my teeth and take one quick swipe at my eyes with the sleeve from my pajamas. Bawlin' like a goddamn baby—how much lower are they gonna make me go, Marge, this place, goddamn old age?

"You and Rachel never thought about going to a lawyer, making out living wills and powers of attorney?"

"Up here in 'God's country'? You gotta be kidding. Besides, Rachel thought she'd die in her bed after a day of hoeing in her garden." I look over at Rachel's spirit. She nods. "People like her don't sign contracts, they trust people."

Woulda, coulda, shoulda. "And that's just not something people talked about in our day. Hell, we could have signed a living will at the White House and Marge would have got a judge to give her custody. This isn't San Francisco."

"So Marge is with Rachel all the time?" The kid's looking at me real intense.

"I guess she goes home at night. I'm so afraid Rachel's gonna die alone, late at night, slip away quiet. That would be her way. But I know deep down she wants me there."

Rachel's spirit gives me that look. "Don't be too sure."

"You're so funny." The kid squints at me. I nod over at the Rachel she can't see. "She's being funny."

You gotta give it to the kid. She just acts like I'm behaving perfectly normal and plows on. "The nurse told me you can visit up here twenty-four hours a day if you want to."

"Nobody wants to." Ain't that the truth? The old lady with the stuffed dolly rolls by my doorway again, muttering about where'd all these bees come from and swatting at the air.

"But I could. Come visit you. Late tonight." The kid leans forward, eyes all lit up, on fire. "And we could take a little stroll over to the other wing, to Rachel's room." She grins and winks. She really does look like a young Natalie Wood, only with more sense of humor. But hell, right this minute I'd be in love with her if she looked like the Jolly Green Giant. She's gonna take me to see Rachel.

"You'd have to help me out of bed. How's your back, kid?"

"Oh, I'm in good shape." She dribbles an imaginary ball for me. Cute. "I play basketball in the winter, softball in the summer."

I look over at Rachel, and the lines at the corners of my eyes crinkle and deepen. I'm laughing without laughing out loud. It's like the kid just drove by on a Harley in full leather in a gay pride parade.

Rachel nods a silent, "You're right. You win."

"How come, kid? How come you're helping us out?"

"Maybe so somebody'll help me out when I get old."

"Don't count on it." I snort. The kid laughs, getting a kick out of me. Now this is more like it, more like me, cranky old grizzly bear not that blubbering baby I was a couple minutes ago.

"So tonight, Hannah?"

"The sooner the better."

She pulls on her sweatshirt. I say goodbye to Bette Midler. "I'll be here. Three o'clock?"

"I'm not going anywhere."

Babydoll grins. "You are tonight, Hannah." She points a finger at me like it's a gun and shoots me. "It's a date."

I finger shoot her back. "It's a date."

And off she goes. God, I'd kill to have knees and hips that worked like that. I find myself watching her ass. I can't help it.

Rachel's spirit steps in close and would slug me if she could. "It's a date," she grumbles and is about to give me a piece of her mind when the kid pops her head back in the door.

"I forgot to ask. Is there anything I can bring you, Hannah? Anything you need?"

"Just Rachel." Rachel's somewhat placated by that. I give her a sweet smile.

The kid's about to leave again when she's almost knocked off her feet by an old geezer on a walker. He's wearing a nice sweater somebody bought him for Christmas, bald, lotsa juice in his legs—lotsa senile folks get strong legs from the juice flowing down insteada up. "You seen my horses?!"

I answer him like he's sensible. "Nope. All we got in here is goats. Old goats. Check down the hall by the water fountain."

"Much obliged, toots." And off he goes, an old farmboy in hot pursuit of his horses.

"He a regular?" The kid watches him peek in another old lady's room, hears the old lady shriek.

"Never seen him before. At least not up here, not bald and eighty. I mighta known him back in the day. Coulda gone to school with him. Well, at least he's got all his parts. There are a couple kids I do recognize up here from the Klee School, all eaten away by time, stumps for legs." I look over at Rachel. "They're the real ghosts."

We watch a nurse's aide lead the old fellow past my door.

"Hope he finds his horses." The kid and me grin at each other then she shoots me with her finger again. "Three o'clock." And off she goes.

Rachel sees me and the kid grin at each other. She crosses

her arms over her chest and looks like tornado season. "It's not like it's the first time you've waved somebody under my nose. That cow Blanche. Your WAC *friend*, what was her name, Jackie? And that fool missionary followed you all the way from Brazil. Brazil!"

America a couple times before, always liked it, kinda the Wild West with samba music. I slipped out of Rachel's bed one night and thumbed my way south—I could afford a plane ticket but where's the adventure in that? I thumbed my way to Galveston, then worked my passage the rest of the way on a banana boat. I wanted the whole trip to be an adventure, meet new people, almost drown—people today on their jet planes miss the trip completely.

In Brazil I did try to behave myself, wire home the money I was making and stay out of the brothels and out of the senoritas. But one morning I was sobering up from helping Brazil celebrate some holiday, napping under a tree, and I woke up to just the swellest little blonde leaning over me, asking me was I okay. She turned out to be this missionary from DeKalb, Illinois, Christina Swedo.

Christina looked at me like I was a lost lamb, so I looked as hangdog and lost as I could manage, and she invited me to lunch at the mission. Lucky (or unlucky) for me she was the only missionary in residence just then—some older couple was up the Amazon seeing if they could convert some cannibals or offer themselves up as a tasty lunch. So there poor little tasty Christina was, ministering to anybody who'd let themselves be ministered to and downright giddy at the prospect of talking English with somebody.

Rachel's kinda churchy, so I have a weakness for ladies who put on a prim exterior—once you get underneath, they got pent-up heat like you can't imagine.

Christina cooked up some thick, meaty soup and we talked all afternoon about this and that until we found ourselves sitting on the couch looking out at the sunset. Christina'd just confessed to me how she'd almost married a good Christian boy from Wheaton College, but she couldn't stand his clammy grip. She'd almost heave when he'd put a moist hand to her cheek and profess his love for her and Jesus, not in that order.

So I put a nice, dry woman's hand to her cheek and stroked

it. She colored up but she didn't pull away. Before she lost her nerve, I leaned in and kissed Christina deep, pulling her up against me, breast to breast, and holding her tight while I stroked her tongue with mine. She let me and she liked it, but I could tell she didn't have much experience in what to do next. Mr. Clammy Hands had obviously left her uninitiated.

I nuzzled her ear and let my hands wander down to her round little ass. To be truthful, I was on pause, giving myself a minute to think without appearing to. This thirty-year-old woman was obviously intact as a twelve-year-old girl who doesn't ride horses. Should I show her a few things or would it be kinder to leave her alone? Kinder and safer? She'd been waiting a long time and had no idea how much fun her body could be. What if I cut her loose from her moorings and then off I'd go and she'd be left here alone with nobody to help her with her needs? Or worse yet, she'd expect me to stay. Thirty-year-old virgins are a sacred responsibility and probably not one a rolling stone like me oughta take on.

That said, I couldn't resist. And I didn't totally drive her away from God. She called out for him quite often that first night and in the nights that followed.

Naturally I moved on with the season, but Christina came along, following me from Brazil to Argentina to Costa Rica to Cuba and finally back to the States. And I have to admit I enjoyed her enthusiasm. It rained our last day in Cuba, a heavy, sultry, tropical rain, so I bought a bottle of wine and rented a small hotel room that smelled of the Caribbean, pineapple and cinnamon and old men's cologne. That afternoon I finally showed my missionary the missionary position, wet to wet as the rain poured down on the palm trees outside our hotel.

We parted company in Tampa. She had a sister in Punta Gorda, and I was lonely for Rachel. I needed to get home for the spring to help her plant her garden. I dearly loved watching Rachel upended planting those rows of corn.

I know, I know. Some people don't believe you can love one woman all your life from the bottom of your soul but

share bodies and beds with other women—well, maybe you can't.

I caught a ride home to Michigan with a couple of Florida snowbirds, a sweet old couple who couldn't stay awake worth beans so I did most of the actual driving. They were amazed by how fast we made the trip and waved goodbye as they inched their car into reverse after dropping me off in Rachel's driveway. I snuck in the front door and caught Rachel at the sink, doing her supper dishes. I had her down on the floor before she knew what hit her. She was pissed at me, but she couldn't bring herself to push me off.

"Hannah, you said you'd be home last month." She tried to keep me from traveling her body, but in no time my face was buried between her legs on the kitchen linoleum.

"God, my god." She tried to talk, but the words kept getting smothered in her throat by the moans. "You promised—you promised you'd install—god—new toilet. Oh Jesus. Dave's running—running—oh Jesus, jeezus..." Rachel was trying to tell me my brother Dave was running for county treasurer and I should help him out with his campaign, put up posters, hand out flyers and some beers at the local tavern, but Dave's campaign was just going to have to wait. So would her new toilet.

We finally made it upstairs to her bedroom. Mixed up in our lovemaking I swear Rachel sniffed me all over like a birddog. Rachel could smell other women on me like my dog Duchess could sniff out a pheasant.

She wouldn't talk to me for a couple days after that. She knew. But after a couple days of stony silence and cold pancakes, we moved on like we always did, because I came home to her.

What about missionary Christina? I spotted her once years later on the arm of a crew cut stone butch sax player in Greenwich Village. I like to think she was glad I brought her out. Clammy-handed men and Jesus weren't her destiny, at

least I hope not. She didn't see me that night in the Village—or she pretended not to. I left it at that.

Well, that was quite a trip down memory lane I just took in my head, all in a split second lyin' in my bed at the Home with spirit Rachel giving me a real suspicious look.

"Hannah, I hope you're thinking about me."

"Always." I smile.

She knows I'm fulla shit, but she appreciates the lie. "You think that girl's going to write you up in her college paper?"

"How could she resist?" My eyes are twinkling because I know how deep the shit's getting. "She's a cute little thing. I bet anything she's like us."

"Well, that's her business. Some things are private."

"You mean hidden. You always were one to pull the curtains." I get my back up pretty quick on this topic and so does Rachel. It's an old, old debate between the two of us. I can see her jaw stiffen and she folds her arms across her chest, but I keep talking. "Hiding. Pretending. Your late husband's photograph on the mantel and flowers on his grave every Decoration Day. You'd plant red geraniums in his urn and visit with all the other good widows, then you'd come home and climb back in bed with me."

"I can't talk to you. I never could." Rachel's really steamed, green eyes on fire—which still makes my heart race same as it did when I was eighteen and she was furious with me. She stomps her pretty little foot at me. "I'm going back to my room."

"Fine." We glower at each other some more, but I break first. "Sorry. Stay. Please."

The "please" gets her. She'd give me a chummy nudge with her elbow if she wasn't a spirit and could.

I give her my best old coot's approximation of a rakish wink. "Used to be we'd make up by doin' the deed."

"Hannah, that time is long past."

"I still feel it. I still want you same as I always did."

31

"Not the way I am now, up here plugged in like a lamp."
The woman can make me laugh and horny hot all at the same time. I grin, but she's looking serious. "Hannah, I really don't want you to see."

"You'll always be the same to me." And it's the truth.

I'm enjoying Rachel so much I'm royally pissed when that damn nurse with the turquoise earrings, that Cleo, bursts in with a goddamn enema bag, jarring me back into right where I am, this goddamn, godforsaken nursing home. "It's that time again, Hannah!"

Rachel discreetly disappears with a kiss to her fingertips and a wave.

I'm not deaf and I don't need that goddamn enema bag the nurse is wagging in my face like a puppy to pet. "I haven't eaten anything. I don't need cleaning out if I haven't eaten anything." Arms folded across what's left of my chest, I treat this funhouse Florence Nightingale to a simmering glare. And I am pissed, so pissed at her and this place and me and old age and losing control of my bowels and my life. I aim all my anger and frustration at Nurse Cleo because she's handy.

She just ignores me anyway; goes about her business with that damn red enema bag. "Hannah, we do this every three days. It's on your chart."

"But I'm not bound up, dammit!"

"That's thanks to this." She cheerfully wags that goddamned enema bag.

"My body's gonna forget how to shit on its own if you keep shoving that tube up me." I jerk away from her hands.

That makes her drop the chart she's tucked under her arm, which finally gets her attention—and makes her grouchy. "Look, we don't want to have to restrain you, Hannah."

"Just try it." I been in my share of bar fights in my time, tough dykes, longshoremen, always held my own. How to fight, being willing to fight, throw a sucker punch, it's not all gone, so Cleo better watch her ass. "I have my mind. I know what I need."

But she won't listen. "Doctor knows what's best for you."

I pull my sheet away from her; hold my PJs close. "I haven't seen that little asshole in three months. How does he know what I need?"

She's gritting her teeth. I'm getting to her—not in a good way but at least I'm getting to her. She's listening to me. Finally. "Hannah, I don't make a fortune doing this. I've got enough on my plate without having to argue with you. I don't have the time."

"Make the time dammit!" I jerk away from her again as she's trying to get at me with that damn tube. "There's more to taking care of people than reaming them out every other day. Don't I have any rights?"

And damned if she doesn't look me right in the eye and say, "No."

Chapter Four

RACHEL

Hannah's sleeping, a deep, angry sleep, snorting and snoring. Hannah's always been a regular brass band to sleep next to—if they'd wanted me to come out of my coma, they should have put her in bed with me for a night or two. I swear the woman could wake the dead.

Not that I'm dead. Not quite. I'm fading, but I can still dream and remember same as her. I just don't usually write it down like she does. I like my privacy. And I don't feel compelled to leave words behind so people will remember me after I'm gone. People pass, years go by, eventually the graves go untended. No one fills the urn come Decoration Day. It's as natural as breathing. But Hannah wants us to be remembered.

Since you're going to have to put up with her side of things through most of this story, I'd like to put in my two cents' worth.

I first noticed Hannah at a Fourth of July parade in town when we were little girls. She was just a blur, chasing after this collie dog of hers, rolling around in the dirt fighting a boy who threw a stone at her. Then she was up and running beside the parade, marching next to the band, running beside the saddle ponies, saluting a dashing young World War I doughboy who was marching with the tottering Civil War veterans. I caught glimpses of her all day, yellow braids flying, and I was just fascinated. Compared to Hannah Free, all the other boys and girls were vanilla ice cream and she was a chocolate sundae with crushed walnuts and a cherry on top.

So that was my misfortune and my salvation to fall under that crazy little tomboy's spell and never fall out of it. Everyone else who tried to get my attention, even my husband, just disappeared like blurry figures in a Kodak. All I could see was Hannah Free. There she was, my Hannah, hanging by her knees or walking the ridge pole of a barn roof, or as a girl barely grown wearing a man's fedora and her brother's trousers, waving to me as she swung up onto a freight train and rolled out of sight.

Yes, I did marry someone else, and I don't regret it. Marriage gave me a house, children, and blessed escape from my parents' house where it was so hard to breathe. And Mr. Johnson's untimely demise gave me a widow's freedom. Of course, I shudder to think how I would have stood forty years with the man, especially after I'd been with my Hannah who knew exactly how to touch me.

After the wedding ceremony, after the cake, I looked for her but I knew she was gone, gone far away, maybe gone for good. So I cleaned up after the guests and then walked into Mr. Johnson's house he'd inherited from his aunt and I locked myself in the bathroom, laid down in the tub, and cried. And cried. Mr. Johnson kept tapping at the door. Finally, after whiskey gave him courage, he knocked rough and told me

enough was enough, so I came out and got it over with.

I got pregnant a year and a half into the marriage, and that made me as happy as anything could.

When I was quite pregnant, Hannah's brother Harold brought by a case of canned salmon Hannah'd caught and canned herself in Alaska. He said she'd sent a case for her ma and one for me. Harold never met my eyes when he carried that case inside and down to the cellar for me. Harold was a rural mail carrier who got killed a few years later misjudging a train and his car's acceleration on some tracks outside town. Kind of a befuddled fellow, a late baby by nearly a month—Hannah's mother said she'd overcooked him. But he meant no harm to anyone and was missed when he crossed over.

Harold tipped his cap as he left to deliver the other case of salmon to his ma. I wasn't sure how to explain the salmon to Mr. Johnson, but he was notable for his lack of curiosity and never asked. I took a long time eating each can, treasuring every bite, imagining Hannah'd caught each salmon herself, picturing her with the wind mussing what hair she had left after a trip to the barber, hoping she was warm enough up there in all that ice and snow.

She'd be wearing her brother Dave's old undershirt and a large navy and red flannel shirt of her stepfather's, both for the warmth and to hide her bosoms. (Trust me, nothing could hide those bosoms.) Brother Harold gave her his peacoat from his service in the navy, and she wore that coat until it was tattered beyond even my patching. I pictured her in Alaska in that peacoat. It's a wonder the men in her family had a stitch to wear. Hannah'd aim those twinkly blue eyes and admire that peacoat or Dave's hip waders and nobody could resist her.

Hannah was gone quite a while before she even wrote to tell me where she'd gone. The salmon was my first present from her, so I was glad to know she still thought of me even if her idea of a romantic gift was tins of fish.

Well, if a case of salmon was good enough for Hannah's ma, I figured it was good enough for me as Hannah prized

Beatrice Freed above all else (well, Bea and me).

Hannah knew she was lucky to be born to a practical woman who accepted her for who she was and never begged her to change. She didn't even mind that the baby girl she named Mary Hannah Freed renamed herself as soon as she could talk, if you believe Hannah. I think old Bea got a real kick out of her tomboy daughter, called her a "character," and personally bailed her out of jail after a particularly ugly fight at the fairgrounds—Hannah hadn't started it, but she'd ended it. It said a lot to people to see her ma take her side like that.

Old Bea never had a girly daughter to pass all her knitting skills on to, so she unofficially adopted me to teach. I think it was the best way she had of making me family. Hannah has her sturdy build and her Scandinavian blond hair (now white), but she sure didn't inherit Bea's live-and-let-live calm disposition.

Not that I was exactly a sea of calm those years Hannah was in Alaska. Before I decided to eat that salmon I almost threw it in the lake. I was furious she was gone. Furious not to hear her rap on my window at night or be able to watch her act the clown just to make me laugh. Furious not to find her sleeping in my porch swing in the dawn light, knapsack under her head for a pillow, dusty from the road, eyes twinkling as she suggests we go find some cows to milk...

I hover over her bed in the nursing home, watching her sleep, a little quieter now, dreaming better dreams.

I don't know how this out-of-body thing works exactly. I heard somebody talk about it on the television years ago and thought it was a load of baloney. But here I am, floating back and forth from my room to hers, seen only by her. I don't know how I do it, but I'm glad I can. I need to see her.

Since she's sleeping peacefully now, I drift back to my room in the blink of an eye and look down on some old woman who can't be me but is. A middle-aged woman who's too old to be my daughter Marge but is sits next to the bed puzzling over a

crossword puzzle. Hannah used to do crosswords in ink, but Marge doesn't have Hannah's vocabulary. Hannah was always reading and she loved the movies. And, of course, she picked up a lot in her travels—she knows enough Spanish and Greek to get by in most restaurant kitchens (that's one of her jokes). Marge reads recipes and the Bible, the harsh parts anyway, so she's not a natural at crossword puzzles. Oh look, she got one. Eight down, *crocus*. Well, good for her.

I birthed Marge and her brother Roy at home during a snowstorm. The doctor got his Ford hung up in a snowdrift, so a neighbor lady, Edna Hutchinson, wallowed through the snow and handled the delivery. She'd been a farmgirl before she moved to town and she'd always helped her pa with the calving. She claimed helping me wasn't much different. Being someone's neighbor went pretty deep in those days.

Mr. Johnson showed off our twins and handed out cigars to his chums, but he was dead before Marge and Roy had any memory of him. His company threw a picnic on board an excursion boat on the lake the summer after the twins were born. I couldn't go because Roy had a fever. Lucky for me because all those poor fools rushed to one side of the boat to wave goodbye and the boat capsized. Many died in the water, weighed down by wet party clothes. Weak swimmers like Mr. Johnson were taken by the lake, swallowed whole.

I rowed the lake for days after, searching for his body to bury. Finally, some boys out frogging found Mr. Johnson bobbing in the lily pads and they ran for me. They helped me tie ropes to him and pull him to shore for a proper burial.

In those days there wasn't any Social Security, so a widow's life could be pretty tough. And I had babies to feed. Somebody must have written Hannah, but it wasn't me. I'd be darned if I'd run crying to her with my sad story. She left me. She could stay gone. But somebody let her know, probably her brother Dave who never knew what to make of us but chose to love Hannah rather than judge her.

Hannah sent me money right away, which I hated to take, but did. But she didn't come back right away. I wondered if she would. I hoped.

It took her a while to finish up her commitments in Alaska. Hannah always was industrious. Most people couldn't find work in the Thirties, but she was always working at three or four jobs. In Alaska she flew hunters into the interior, taught school, which still makes me laugh, did some bootlegging. She even started a fish canning business with that Nettie Bobo and that business is still in operation and sending her checks. So she had things to see to before she could leave, but then I swear she took her sweet time getting here. Knowing her she didn't pay for passage. I'm sure she fished and cowboyed and thumbed her way home. She said she wasn't sure she'd be welcome.

I was baking and doing wash for the banker's wife when Hannah turned up at my kitchen door. Seeing her was—well, I don't want to get all mushy, but it was a strong feeling washed over me, fury mixed with just the deepest contentment mixed with heat. But you don't need to hear about that from me. Hannah will be glad to tell all and show you the Polaroids.

After that Hannah came and went, off on her adventures and her business ventures—like I say, the woman was good at making money when no one else was. Of course, she'd do anything.

She spent an entire fall riding shotgun on a pinball delivery truck as a favor to her brother Rudy after Sheriff Amble caught him with a still and threw him in jail. Hannah usually worked at honest jobs, but I think she enjoyed pretending to be an outlaw that one fall. I worried about her, but she claimed she only had to point that shotgun at one of those horse thieving, dognapping Blackledges, and he backed down.

Even if she did always wear pants, I wouldn't say Hannah was a father figure, or a mother figure, to my kids, but she was good to Marge and Roy. She sent them presents and postcards

when she was gone, one year the Eiffel Tower, the next the Pyramids. Hannah showed Roy how to fish for walleye and hit a golf ball, and she sat up with Marge when it stormed. She sent Roy a baseball signed by several Brooklyn Dodgers and Marge got moonflower seeds from South America.

And she always came back. Just when I had myself convinced I'd never see Hannah Free again, in she'd come.

Chapter Five

HANNAH

Why am I dreaming about golfing with Roy? What a waste of dreaming. But there we are, swinging our clubs. Never had much use for cow pasture pool, but I was pretty good at it, so we'd go out when he'd come home from California every couple years to visit his mother.

Living in California, Roy didn't have any issues about Rachel and me—he said he'd seen it all out there in Modesto—but he also didn't care so deep as Marge. Roy was always pretty wrapped up in sports, then the Marines, and eventually his drywall business and a couple of wives and kids. He'd call Rachel every few weeks, loved her in a kinda dull, uninvolved way that reminded her of Mr. Johnson. I never could decide which I'd rather have, Mr. Hands Off or Marge who loved Rachel too much and was never satisfied with her.

So here I am dreaming of Roy landing another ball in the

water hazard out to Devil's Knob golf course—those Johnson men never had good luck with water. Every course we ever played, water was a magnet for Roy and his Top- Flite balls. And he'd wade in and find everybody's ball but his.

I close my eyes and open them looking up into big, white, fluffy clouds, and I wish I could wade right up into them—probably why I loved flying; it was a way to wade the clouds. I look to see how Roy's doing with his balls, but I've dream drifted right up to Rachel's bed in her bedroom at home, which is exactly where I want to be, so I can wade into her fluffy white sheets...

"Hannah? Hannah, wake up. Hannah, wake up, you overslept."

Dammit, I don't want to wake up. I want to keep dreaming and slip into bed with Rachel and wake *her* up.

But when I grudgingly open my eyes, it's that kid in a black turtleneck like she's James Bond, and tight black jeans—her spy clothes. It's three o'clock in the morning. She's here to take me to see Rachel. I'll finally get to see Rachel. I wake up.

"It's time to go see Rachel. The coast is clear." She shakes me gently, pulling away the blanket, an old Indian blanket I bought in Florida on one of my first trips out of Michigan. I'd wanted to see a palm tree and rassle an alligator, and I got to do both, not to mention eat my weight in grouper and grapefruit. The blanket reminds me of better times. I can almost taste the grapefruit and see the pelicans. I'm glad this damn Home lets us bring a few personal touches. Wouldn't let me bring my moose head though. Food's terrible. Wish I could fry me up a nice grouper over a campfire by the Gulf of Mexico...

"Hannah. Hannah, you're falling back to sleep. Wake up. The nurse is listening to her Walkman. It's the perfect time to slip by her and on over to Rachel's room. Do you need to use the bathroom first?"

Somehow she's got me propped up, feet dangling off the bed. I feel weak as a kitten. I hate this, hate needing help for every goddamned thing, even taking a piss. "Sorry. Yes, I do."

Bless her heart, she's jolly about it. Says she always has to go when she wakes up. She slips my feet into some slippers I've never seen before.

"These aren't my slippers."

"I bought you a new pair."

I give her a hard squint in the dim light. "Are you adopting me?"

"Maybe." She gives me that cute little half smile.

"You are hard up."

I see Rachel's spirit over the kid's shoulder. She's looking kinda miffed, jealous. Poor Rachel—it's not like I didn't give her reason. "Hannah, don't you let that girl go in the bathroom with you."

"Get a grip on yourself." We enjoy scowling at each other.

"Take a good grip on me, Hannah. I'll help you into your chair." The kid's not very big but she does have a good grip on her—all that softball.

"Just move the chair closer, kid. I can get into it."

Rachel smiles. "You're always so darn independent."

The kid smiles. "Are you always so damn independent?"

"Just move the chair closer." I sound gruff, but it's just because I'm so grateful I'm in danger of turning to mush. "I appreciate this."

The kid nods, her strong hands on my arm and back, guiding me into the chair. "I know."

It was a little hair-raising sneaking me down the hall, into the elevator, and down another well-lit hallway. Lucky one nurse was away from her nurses station and the night nurse on Rachel's floor was reading a romance novel and listening to her Walkman.

But finally here we are. And there she is. Rachel, hair still long and barely gray at seventy-nine; Rachel lying still as death in that hospital bed, IV, feeding tube, oxygen, the works, enough electricity and machinery to run a small dairy farm, all

just to keep her from leaving us. I'm so glad to see her, but it breaks my heart. The kid pushes me close to the bed, so I can hold Rachel's hand, then she steps away, discreet.

So I take Rachel's hand in mine for the thousandth time. "Poor baby. Go ahead and sleep. I just wanna be here."

I can sense her spirit watching me, us, but I don't look around to see if I see her. That would be just too eerie, making eye contact with a thirty-year-old Rachel while I'm finally holding my old sweetheart's hand and getting to pet real hair and admire every wrinkle she says I gave her.

I find myself talking to the kid as I hold Rachel's dear hand in mine and stroke her face. "We were in love all our lives, but the last years were the best of the best. You know, even if you don't say it, that it's not going to last forever, so you stop bickering over every little thing and treasure every tuna casserole you eat together. And those last years Rachel stopped hiding so much and I stayed home." I look at Rachel, so still in the bed. "After all my years wandering, I finally learned where my home is."

It's a nice moment—and then it's over because the damn night nurse walks in, Agnes of the Walkman and the romance novels. She looks worn out, but she moves faster than you'd think.

"What's going on here? Hannah? Hannah, what are you doing in here? How in the world did you even get yourself here?" She's reaching to grab onto the back of my wheelchair. "Let's take you back to your room. You know how her family feels."

"I'm family!"

We're on the verge of a bloodbath when the kid steps in and lays a big juicy lie on the nurse. "Stop. Let her go. Nurse, I brought Hannah in to see my Great-Grandma Rachel. I take full responsibility."

The nurse and the baby dyke square off. But you can see in the nurse's face that her corns are hurting and this is the last

46

thing she needs at three thirty in the morning. "Who'd you say you are? I haven't seen you here before."

"I just flew in. This is my great-grandmother's room, and Hannah is Great-Grandma Rachel's best friend. Of course, she should be here."

"But that daughter of hers—"

The kid makes ferocious eye contact. "That's why we came so late at night, to give them privacy. We don't want a scene, do we?"

They're toe to toe, Soviets versus the U.S. but finally Kruschev blinks. "Well, fine. But when I do my next bed check in twenty minutes, Hannah had better be gone."

The kid doesn't budge an inch. "We'll leave at dawn. She's not hurting anyone."

The nurse, who's not really such a bad sort, just trying to do the right thing whatever the hell that is, finally rolls her eyes and nods. "Fine. But if that daughter catches you two in here, I didn't see either one of you." And off she goes on her aching corns. Hurray.

I wink at the kid. "What a load of crap. I think I'm rubbing off on you."

"I hope so, Hannah." She gives my shoulder a squeeze and kisses the top of my head, then she settles back down in a visitors chair, out of the way.

I squeeze Rachel's hand. "You hear that, Rachel? I get to stay."

And we do, we stay until dawn. I get to touch Rachel's face, trace the lines with my finger so I'll remember every one and can feel her on my hands even when I'm back in my own bed. I love and hate every minute of this visit. I know this isn't what Rachel'd want, lying here trapped in her own body, machines doing her breathing for her. We never really talked about it. We didn't have to. I just know. And so would she if it was me in that bed. How can that damn Marge let her go on like this? She probably thinks she's doing it out of love, but it's selfish.

47

Chapter Six

GRETA

Hannah keeps calling me "kid," which is lucky. If it ever occurs to her that she doesn't know my name and I tell her then she'll know the truth and what if she hates me? She probably won't, but she might. What if she does?

I'm pretty tired, so my mind's racing. I'm mulling this over as I'm listening to the old guy who was looking for his horses. Turns out he was in the Civilian Conservation Corps—I really am writing a paper, a senior thesis on the Depression, so this CCC shit is right up my alley. This old guy may be pretty fuzzy on current events, but he has a very firm grasp on 1934, so I sit with him and listen. He likes it when I take notes.

We're sitting on a couch in the activities room at the Home. A couple of old ladies are drinking coffee at the one table. There's a fireplace that doesn't work, a few ferns, a not very flattering painting of Jesus, somebody's shoe, and a black cat

sleeping in the window. There's a senile old babe painting at an easel behind us. She's good. Her brain may be mush, but it can still guide her hand to paint a really pretty landscape. Maybe that's what's in her head, rolling meadows and streams—beats this dump. Same for my old cowpoke who's happy living in the past. Beats living here.

When I notice that lost shoe in the corner, I look down to see if he's got both of his. He fixes me with an intense stare. I better pay attention.

"Yessir, I was in the CCCs. Planted rows and rows of trees. Lotta discipline. Just like bein' in the military. Good preparation for WW Two."

I nod attentively, jot notes. "So what did you do when the war ended?"

"What d'ya mean ended?"

Ah. He's still living in 1943, still driving a jeep for a colonel in D.C. None of his buddies have died yet at Normandy. He's still got a ticket to see Bob Hope and dance with all the girls at the USO. Why wouldn't he rather live in a world where he was still so vitally alive? Man, my Buddhist hippie dad would think I was nuts thinking a world at war was a better place to be.

The old guy taps me on the knee. "Say, aren't you Betty Grable?"

I laugh and am about to give the old fox a peck on the cheek when I hear that dreaded voice.

"Greta?"

There she is. Tightly permed church lady hair, her best dress from about 1962, what could be a pretty face all tight and pruney from decades of disapproving of just about everything. I managed to avoid her yesterday, but today my luck has run out. Grandma Marge, purse tight to her chest, is standing in the doorway looking me right in the eye. She's more surprised than I am. And I don't give her much. "Yup."

"I had no idea you were in town." She's bewildered. Glad to see me, a little hopeful, but cautious. Last time we saw each other, at my Mom's funeral, I wasn't exactly friendly. "Weren't

you planning to come see me?"

"Nope." I glare at her.

The old fellow's watching us like we're the new act at the stage door canteen. "Are you a friend of Betty's?"

"Betty?" Marge is bewildered again.

I look at her like she's pretty dim—which she is. "Betty Grable." I give the old soldier a peck on the cheek. "Sir, I would like you to meet Tallulah Bankhead."

He's tickled. "What kind of a name is Tallulah?"

"I'm sure it's an insult." Grandma Marge gives me that martyred look I bet she's worked on all her life. I'm not buying it.

I ignore her and shake the old guy's hand. "Thanks for talking to me, sir."

He can't remember he did. The CCCs, the war years, all fading. "Have you seen my horses?" he bellows right in Marge's face.

She jumps a foot. "Why no."

I point out at the hallway. "I think they went thataway."

"Much obliged." He gives me a wink. "Save me a dance." And off he goes, giving Marge a wide berth, like you would a rattlesnake.

Grandma forces a tight smile and tries to act like everything's normal. "Greta, are you staying in town long?"

"As long as I want."

She pouts. "Must you be so rude?"

"I think I must." I turn away and start gathering my pad and pens into my knapsack. I bend to pick up a dropped pen and look over at a handsome old man dozing over a chess board. Before he fell asleep, he told me he thought his name was Baron. The painter lady is now adding what looks like a Paris street scene to her landscape, all of it alive in her memory. Total concentration. She has no idea we're here—lucky her.

Grandma Marge is pouting, on the verge of tears. I don't care. "I guess it's nice you've at least come to see your great-grandmother."

"Sure. Her I like." I can't stop myself. Here it comes. "And

I missed out on ever really knowing her because of that stupid fight you had with Mom."

"That man—your father—" Marge stops herself but it's a little late.

"I know, I know. You didn't approve of Daddy, because he was a Buddhist and a community activist. Mom told me. She didn't want to, but I kept asking her when we were going to go back to Michigan again so I could fish and drink hot chocolate and go to the fair with those nice old ladies, Hannah and Rachel. So mom had to tell me. She said you and she were no longer speaking. And now you've lost your chance, because she's dead." That was too mean. I wish I could take it back. Maybe saying rotten, stupid things runs in the family.

Grandma Marge looks like she's been slapped in the face, but she stands there and takes it like a good Christian martyr. "Greta, I wish I could take it back. I would if I could."

"Then why are you doing the same damn thing to Hannah and Rachel?"

She's shocked that I know. "This isn't the same thing. This isn't the same thing at all."

I don't say anything. I just sling my knapsack over my shoulder and prepare to make my getaway. I want to go sit with Hannah. She's home for me.

"Come to lunch?" You've got to give Grandma Marge credit. She hangs in there.

"Sure. Maybe I'll even bring my lover. She likes a good lunch."

We trade silent glares.

"Is this a test, Greta?"

"It's just the truth." Another dyke in the family, a chip off the old block, Rachel and Hannah's true great-grandchild.

"Why am I not surprised?" She fumbles with her purse.

"Yeah, why aren't you surprised? You just knew I'd turn out bad with my draft-card burning Buddhist father and my wonderful vegetarian Democrat of a mom. Naturally I was doomed to be a goddamn queer."

Now Marge is the one turning to leave. "I'd better get back. I like to make sure they turn Mom often enough. So she doesn't get bedsores."

"You're making the same mistake, Grandma. The same mistake all over again. And you're hurting them both."

"It's not the same thing." She stands there, echoing the same mantra, rooted in the same old shit. "It's not the same thing at all."

So I shake my head and leave the room first.

I grew up in Minneapolis, an only child because my folks really believed population control started with them. But they took in foster kids and some of those kids were with us for years, until they grew up, so I consider them family and they call me "little sister." A bunch of them came to my parents' funerals and told me how moving in with us saved their lives. It's a shame Marge couldn't appreciate what good people my folks were. They really practiced what they preached. I don't want to paint them as perfect—Dad missed making it to quite a few of my soccer matches because of his fondness for weed and Mom had her martyr moments—but all-in-all they were a pretty honorable old pair of hippies. Of course, their idea of dressing up was jeans and a Grateful Dead T-shirt, so I guess it's no wonder Marge couldn't appreciate them.

I remember when I was real little us taking a couple of trips to Michigan to visit my mom's family. They called her Barbara. Everyone in Minneapolis called her Bobbie, so the Barbara thing confused me at first. She and Grandma Marge were pretty stiff with each other, so I was glad when we spent time with Marge's mom, Rachel, and her friend, Hannah.

I thought Hannah was a man at first. She wore men's clothes and always seemed to be hammering nails, patching the roof, or fixing the brake lines on her old car. And she swore like a sailor, which was one of the dozens of things she'd been. But she was pretty in a weathered kind of way, and her breasts

55

swung heavy under her old flannel shirts, so I got the idea she was some kind of magical woman. And Hannah was early evidence that Mom was right when she said girls could do anything boys did including fix their own brakes. I suppose she learned that watching Hannah herself when she was a girl.

When Mom and Marge got into it over Daddy (who wasn't along that trip because he was in jail—antinuke protest), Rachel tried to referee but ugly things got said and no one apologized. When Hannah could see things were going from bad to worse, she leaned down to me and said, "Let's you 'n me go fishing."

So we did. She even let me row and showed me how to bait my hook. We caught a nice mess of bluegill and sunfish, but I never got to eat them, because when we got back, Mom had the car packed. And off we went. She drove for hours, like she wanted to be sure she got far enough away.

And we never came back. Grandma Rachel sent me Christmas and birthday cards with five dollars in them, but Mom and Marge never exchanged another word. I wonder if they kept thinking they'd make up some day, that some day one of them would reach out, make the first move, but then Mom died.

I was in college, junior year, when my parents were in a head-on collision—whiteout conditions, a drunk driver (who lived). Dad died immediately, but Mom was in the hospital for several days, kept alive by a jungle of wires and machinery, like Rachel. It was up to me, but I knew what she'd want. Knowing what's right and actually pulling the plug are two different things, but I finally willed myself to kiss her goodbye and let her go. When I'd turned eighteen, Mom had papers filled out, will, living will, power of attorney, the works, leaving everything to me and putting me in charge if anything happened to them. Mom was careful that way. And she didn't trust Marge. Hell, I barely knew Marge. I had to dig all over to find her phone number. But I waited to have the hospital call her until after

I'd pulled the plug. Maybe that was cruel, but I was trying to do what I thought Mom would want.

Marge and I barely spoke at the funeral. Mom's friends and mine stayed close to me while Marge sat by herself. Grandpa Mason had the flu, so they wouldn't let him fly. He had to miss the funeral. So there she sat by herself. I feel bad that I didn't feel bad. Not about Marge.

It was so sudden. how could my parents be dead? I felt like I was drowning.

The only way I got through those months was having an English prof of mine, Robyn, take me to dinner and movies and plays and threaten me if I didn't make it to class. It's a small liberal arts college. Everyone knew what had happened. I'd taken several classes from Robyn—well, every class she taught—so she knew me well enough to reach out. And she didn't intend it to be more.

But once I wasn't in a class of hers anymore—I knew she was too honorable to cross that line—once grades were in, I reached out to her.

She'd just ended a fifteen-year relationship that reeked of lesbian bed death. Her former partner was "age appropriate" but an alcoholic who never finished her own PhD. and hated that Robyn had. Lots of resentment.

So, badly burned, Robyn had no intentions, no expectations when she befriended me—she was honestly just being nice. Which I found really attractive. And one night after a bottle of wine and a fabulous Gena Rowlands movie, *A Woman Under The Influence*, I simply refused to go home. Robyn tried to be the mature one. Looked exasperated—which only made her more endearing.

So I kissed her. She tried to pull away so I kissed her again and pushed her up against the wall of her kitchen so she couldn't back away. I could tell nobody'd kissed her in a long time—that fifteen years with the resentful drunk really did stink of lesbian bed death. I slipped my hands up under Robyn's sweatshirt and was thrilled to find no bra, just lovely

large breasts that hadn't been cupped by a lover's hands in a really long time.

Robyn gasped and I kissed her deeper. I had my fingers in the elastic of her sweatpants and was about to fuck her against the wall when she suddenly got up her nerve and picked me up off the floor (Robyn's a big gal) and started kissing me back—and she sure remembered how.

After several minutes Robyn carefully set me back down on the floor. "Who is seducing whom here?"

"Let's take turns." Wow. I was so proud of myself. What a perfect thing to say.

And that was the last thing either of us said for hours except to occasionally moan out a traffic direction, higher, lower, deeper, faster, I'm sorry I'm so wet, I'm not sorry...

I walk into Hannah's room. She's sleeping. She's smiling in her sleep. I bet she's dreaming of Rachel. So I prop up my feet and lean back in the visitors chair and hope I dream of Robyn.

Chapter Seven

HANNAH

Someone's in the room, but I don't want to open my eyes, don't want to see that nurse with more pills for me or an old lady looking for her mama or Marge clutching her purse, so I play dead—pretty easy up here.

Eyes closed, I see white. Winter. I loved the winters in Michigan, especially when I was a kid or could act like a kid. I don't suppose I was exactly a steady, stable force in Marge's and Roy's childhoods—I left the parenting to Rachel—but I did show them some fun.

I knew all the best sledding hills from when I was kid, and I'd take Marge and Roy on some wild rides. Marge enjoyed it more than you'd think. She wasn't so buttoned down when

she was a little girl. And Roy loved all that rough and tumble. Neither one of them could ice skate worth a damn, but they loved racing down Tank Hill on that old sled of mine.

Roy even liked to ice fish with my brother Rudy, when Rudy wasn't in jail for poaching deer or running a still or a card game—my Ma once said Rudy's biggest talent was for getting caught. Rachel used to worry whether Rudy was a good influence, but Roy didn't really have the nerve for a life of crime. Not exactly a fireball but in need of a little adult male camaraderie, Roy really liked to sit in that ice shack and stare into that hole in the ice for hours while Rudy spun his stories. Roy'd listen and chuckle and check his line, but he didn't go poach deer with Rudy or gamble. He pretty well stuck to the straight and narrow, got a girl pregnant in high school, joined the Marines, pretty ordinary stuff for a small-town kid.

Now that Marge was a beautiful little girl—she's still a looker if you take a gander underneath all her pissy, righteous anger and that church lady hair. How could she not be gorgeous? She's Rachel's daughter after all. When she was little, she'd hang on me when I'd turn up, like she was afraid I'd disappear any minute. She'd help me till Rachel's garden and ride my shoulders to the store when I'd go for a Sunday paper. We were real buddies, catching fireflies together and watching the moonflowers open at dusk. And in the winter, I'd pick her up and drive her home from school to save her having to climb over the drifts in her good clothes. Roy would be playing king of the mountain or shooting baskets in the gym with the other boys and always got himself home. He and I did our bonding on the lake or in the woods—and squirrels usually died as a result—but Marge really treasured getting those rides home (not many kids got 'em in those days, so it made her feel special, pampered).

But all good things come to an end, right? Eventually Marge started seeing me as an embarrassment. Other kids said things; adults whispered. I'd come to drive her home from

dances, and she'd look just mortified. I think she was relieved when I joined up during the war and wasn't there to mortify her anymore.

Of course, what really drove a stake through our relationship was when Marge started going to the Baptist Church with Rachel's sourpuss ma. That belligerent old babe moved in with Rachel and the kids after Rachel's father rolled a tractor over on himself and that was it for him. Rachel is not an only child, but you'd think she was when it came to the bidding war over who got to take in the old biddy.

She hated me just as much as I hated her. You should've seen her look me over at the breakfast table before she'd pass me the syrup for my pancakes—syrup I probably paid for. She knew Rachel and me did something unspeakable upstairs, but she didn't dare confront Rachel over it and risk losing the sofabed she called home. Rachel might appear soft at first sight, womanly, but when the front door was shut what she did inside her own home was her own damn business, and that old carp knew it, knew her days of bossing Rachel ended the day Rachel married Mr. Johnson to get away from her.

Unfortunately those years old Gertrude lived with Rachel before pneumonia (the old person's friend and mine) carried her away gave Gertrude a chance to get Marge interested in the Baptist Church. We made the mistake of asking Marge to drive the old lady to church a couple of times, and something in those stiff-necked, judgmental Baptists called out to Marge in a way Rachel's kinder, mellower Methodists did not.

By the time I came back from my service in World War II, Marge had married Mason and was singing in the choir at the Baptist Church, and she just barely tolerated me over the Thanksgiving turkey.

I know she said a lot to Rachel over coffee and doughnuts, especially when I was globe-trotting, off to South America or Singapore. And Rachel probably let her vent; put her foot down if Marge got too nasty but otherwise let her talk then

just ignored everything Marge said and went on doing what she pleased. Rachel put a lotta effort into keeping the peace, because she did love Marge and loved being a grandma to Barbara. And Marge had a couple miscarriages and a stillborn after she had Barbara, so Marge needed her mother whether she ever admitted it or not. Trusting and taking comfort in God's Plan had to get harder and harder after every lost baby. She needed Rachel's hand to hold, but all the losses made her more bitter.

She didn't particularly like seeing people happy, especially not her mom and me. Watching Rachel and me go see *From Here To Eternity* together at the movie theater and bet a nickel on the harness races at the county fair just galled her, I know it did. And hearing the gossip and the giggles and the outraged sniffing over coffee hour at church must have reminded Marge of standing on the school steps in her party dress and looking across the parking lot after school dances and seeing me leaning against the hood of my pickup, smoking, waiting to drive her home. I was a lot more embarrassing than the average parent.

What I'm saying is Marge is a royal pain in my ass, but I used to like her when she was a kid, and I can understand how she got to be the way she is.

I'm slipping away into sleepy time picturing Marge and Rachel gardening together—they were both crazy for dahlias. I think as they got older, there was an unspoken truce, an avoiding of certain subjects (i.e., me), letting sleeping dogs lay that let them enjoy each other with a trowel and a flowerpot in their hands. Or they'd talk baking and crochet, trade recipes and compare pumpkin pies—Rachel actually liked using the canned pumpkin best, but Marge enjoyed brutally chopping away at a real pumpkin (figures—lotta animosity in that little woman). Of course, so much for truce when Rachel became incapacitated and found herself in this Home. Marge saw her chance to finally "do what's right" and she took it.

I'm still awake but my eyes are clamped shut, and I'm obsessing when I oughta be in dreamland, dreaming about better days, like the henhouse. That's one of my favorite dreams, favorite memories, kissing Rachel in the henhouse.

We're only eight or ten, so it's pretty innocent. I lean in past her wavy brown hair and kiss Rachel, a big sloppy kiss on the cheek, and she wipes it away, which makes me yell so loud I scare the chickens.

Rachel shushes me, but, bold as brass, I lean in and tell her to kiss me this time. I hold my breath wondering if she will or if she won't and yippee she does. Then she runs off and I'm left to sing of my love for her to the chickens who don't really appreciate my song stylings.

The henhouse was also where we enjoyed our first deep kiss when we were fifteen. If I dream just right, maybe I'll—

Dammit. That fool mail lady half falls on me delivering a letter. Suddenly I'm wide awake and back to being just another cranky old fart in a nursing home. I've managed to never murder anybody yet, so I'm lucky I don't have my deer rifle—so is she. "Goddammit."

"Oops. Sorry, sorry," she chirps, admiring the stamp on my letter.

I look over at the kid, fast asleep in the visitors chair. She must be exhausted, but then I suppose college kids can sleep through anything.

This well-meaning idiot of a mail lady—too much makeup and a stuffed monkey climbing out of her pocket—waves an orange envelope in my face. "More mail, Hannah. My, you are popular. You get more mail than the rest of this place put together."

"That's pretty damn sad." I manage to snatch the envelope from her claws and rip into it.

She tries to peek. "Hallmark?"

"That's for me to know." I tune her out and start to read.

She makes one more lame try, fixing me with that frantically cheery smile. "I wish I knew somebody in New Mexico."

63

"Well, you don't."

She twitters to herself on her way out, but I finally send her packing. A note from Jackie. What a treat.

Oh dang. Rachel's spirit shows up at just the wrong moment. She's seen me rip open that envelope to get at Jackie's letter like it's opium for a dope fiend. Rachel is not pleased. "Who's that from?"

"Just a minute, honey. Thirty seconds." I try to stall and hide the postmark on the envelope.

But she heard that damn mail lady. She knows. "New Mexico?"

"Yes." I'm already on the last paragraph. Jackie writes a good letter but never a long one—she's too busy.

"I'm going to my room." Rachel turns her back to go.

I drop the notecard with its cactus on the cover—not Hallmark—on the bed and give Rachel my full attention. Well almost. I sneak a peek at the kid. It's amazing what she can sleep through. She has her arm flung across her eyes and is whistling through her teeth in her sleep. "I'm listening, Rachel. Don't leave."

"But your mind's in New Mexico."

"That was a long time ago, sweetheart. The war. Lonely days far from home."

Rachel knows me too well. She rolls her eyes. "Bullshit. I was lonely, too."

I can't not laugh. "You know being near death has really brought out your racy side."

"If she's still so crazy about you, why doesn't she visit you?"

"She's busy." I know Rachel doesn't really want to talk about Jackie, but she can't help herself. So I actually try to honor her with a sincere answer. "Besides, I don't think Jackie wants to see me like this. And I'd rather not see me in her eyes. Don't be jealous of her, Rachel. She was no match for you."

I hear the kid's chair squeak and look over. Her eyes are open and I can tell she's been listening to my half of the

conversation. She must think I'm nuts, but she don't seem to mind. I look back over at Rachel, but she's gone. Maybe it's just as well if I'm going to start remembering my time with Jackie.

The kid stretches and takes off to buy an orange juice from the machine. I zonk out in the midst of trying to think what to write back to Jackie. I don't have a lot to tell her that'll compete with all her backpacking and trips to Vegas. "Dear Jackie. We don't do much white-water rafting up to the Home..." I drift off with that line in my head. Dear Jackie...

My dreams obligingly deliver me back to that smoky bar in New Mexico, Glen Miller's "String of Pearls" and the Andrews Sisters' "Don't Sit Under the Apple Tree" on the jukebox, air thick with cigarette smoke. We all smoked back then; all the girls tasted like Marlboros or Lucky Strikes. I was in my uniform, looking across the table at Jackie, this pretty, broad-faced, Irish-looking girl with her Andrews Sisters' hair, so tempting in her WAC uniform. I was paying for the drinks and letting our knees touch under the table. I wasn't rushing her, but I didn't intend to spend the night alone.

Turns out I wasn't her first. She'd gone to a Catholic girls school, and she claimed even some of the nuns were lesbian, but I've never seen a nun who looked happy enough to be a lesbian. Jackie's parents had it in mind that she should be a "bride of Christ" like some sour old Sisters of Mercy aunt of hers, so Jacks joined the Women's Army Corps to give herself some breathing room. She never did go back to the East Coast where she grew up except to visit. She'd found what she needed in New Mexico.

We had to be careful. Discreet. One of us would rent a hotel room, then the other one would sneak up. Or we'd camp. Jackie was one of my longer affairs, which is probably why Rachel sees red when she knows I'm thinking of New Mexico.

That first night we got a hotel room with a radio and

65

danced to Artie Shaw. I liked the slow dances, pressed up close against her, finding my way into her clothing. Jackie even let me lead, unlike Nettie Bobo and half those damn dykes in Alaska.

The feel of her breasts like torpedoes pressing against me as we danced, thighs, nylons whispering under her skirt, I finally couldn't stand it anymore and pushed Jackie down on the bed. I kissed her deep while my fingers fumbled with her garters, all those layers. I was soaking wet by the time I finally got to her panties and slipped first one then a second finger inside her. Then came my tongue.

Jackie grabbed hold of the headboard with both hands when I did that—I guess her Catholic school pals weren't so bold. Their loss. As her hips writhed, I just buried my face deeper in her black, curly snatch and loved listenin' to her come (so did the rest of that hotel).

Stationed all that time in New Mexico, I felt guilty getting letters and socks from Rachel. I knew she missed me, missed my company at her table and in her bed. And she couldn't find relief like I could. And she wouldn't have even if she coulda, not even if some big butch came to her wrapped up in Christmas tinsel. Other than marrying Mr. Johnson, Rachel wasn't one to stray. And I never did either, not in my heart. I could be absolutely faithful to Rachel in my heart while sharing a bed and some wonderful laughs with a sassy, dark-eyed WAC in a hotel in the mountains of New Mexico. If you're not built that way, I can't explain it.

Chapter Eight

RACHEL

She always said, "Well, come with me. Please, Rachel, please come." Please come to Paris. Or Singapore. Or New Mexico. I ask you, how could I with children? And even after they were grown, I wouldn't go away with her. I stayed home where I was the queen of my castle. I couldn't control much in my life, certainly not my emotions, but I did own that yellow frame house with the garden out back. Hannah could and would come and go, but my power came from staying.

Hannah came home from World War II still wearing her uniform. I think she wanted me to see her in it. And she did look so handsome.

I'd gotten concerned this was one time she might stay away, stay out in New Mexico with this "friend" she always

seemed to be having dinner with—trust me, I know what Hannah likes to eat.

I was lying on the couch, afghan over my legs, reading "The Saturday Evening Post" when Hannah came home from the War. I heard the door—I never locked it in those days— and there she was, grinning.

Roy was in the Marines, occupying Japan, and Marge was in her own house, her first house as a married woman, nursing Mason back to health after he came home to her from the South Pacific one leg shorter than the other and missing toes from an explosion. I'd buried my mother. So it was just me in that house when Hannah came home from the War.

I cried just like every other wife whose mate came home to her in one piece, just sobbed and got her uniform all wet, clung to her and kissed her, so happy and relieved I couldn't believe it. And Hannah just kept grinning and holding onto me and letting me bawl my eyes out until I'd finally had my fill and almost shyly took her hand and drew her up the stairs with me, because it had been such a long time and it was a chilly night outside.

I think we stayed in that bed for a week. One of us would get up and feed the chickens or make us a sandwich to share, but then she'd take me in her arms, and we'd discover each other all over again. If you need any more details, you ask her. She's the talker.

Hannah stayed home with me for nearly a year after she came home from the War. Her mother wasn't well, cancer, so we took care of her 'till she died. And admit it or not, I think Hannah was just glad to be home. I made her peanut butter cookies, and she and her brother Dave worked on their fly fishing.

There was such a housing demand after the War, that Hannah and Dave went into business fixing up old houses to sell to returning vets and their pregnant wives. Dave was the best

furnace man in the county, and somewhere Hannah'd learned to wire houses and carpenter new cupboards for kitchens, and they both hated to plumb, hated to fix a toilet, but they could do it. They earned a tidy profit doing the work themselves turning these rundown farmhouses into somebody's dream home. They could even finish it off with a new roof—or patch up the old one good as new.

Hannah patching a roof brought us the closest we ever came to breaking up.

Somewhere along the line, we'd developed this unspoken agreement that what Hannah did with other women outside Michigan, even outside the mid-Michigan area, was her business. I didn't like it, but I guess I did stray first by marrying Mr. Johnson. And over the years I had to face the fact that the big spirit I loved in Hannah was not meant to be starved or denied when she was away. The woman was always hungry.

But without saying anything, we both knew Hannah wasn't supposed to shame me in my own backyard, so she never diddled around in town—except this once.

Her name was Blanche. She was a widow friend of Hannah's mom, sixty years old if she was a day, built like a rouged battleship, all chest and torso and corset. She cornered Hannah at the hardware and got all pitiful nattering on about the leak she had in the roof over her kitchen. There were shingles in her shed—her wheezing old insurance man husband had promised to patch that roof but he kept putting it off till he up and died on her last spring.

Hannah was still feeling vulnerable from losing her mom to the Reaper, feeling a special weakness for old cows mooing in distress (not that her mom was a cow). And Hannah liked playing the hero. So she told this Blanche she'd come over next afternoon and climb her roof. I'd told her I'd be busy over to Marge's—I'd promised to teach Marge how to knit baby booties for this second baby she was, as it turned out, destined to miscarry. So off Hannah went with her tools.

Years later, when I could almost listen without wanting to

kill her, Hannah told me what happened next. After steadying the ladder, that old heifer Blanche watched from the ground while Hannah scrambled around on that roof like a monkey and made it sound again. She even tested her work with the garden hose after she was through. Not a drop leaked through.

After exclaiming over her dry kitchen floor, Blanche offered Hannah an RC Cola in the parlor, but Hannah said she was way too sweaty and dirty for somebody's good furniture. (I admit I get a little fussy about that.)

But I'll bet old Blanche gave her a look that said she appreciated a little honest sweat, that she liked how Hannah's short yellow hair stuck to her forehead and sweat dripped off her chin.

To hear Hannah tell it, she was just innocently taking a big swig of RC in Blanche's front hallway and almost choked when that old viper Blanche pulled her housedress right up over her pin curls and dropped it on the floor at Hannah's feet. I'm not a big woman, but I suspect Hannah likes a fleshy woman when she's looking elsewhere, and there was Blanche filling up every inch of that silky slip, all ready to make Hannah a trade for her labor.

And this pains me to say it, but Hannah did not resist—or didn't resist much. I won't go into the details—I don't know any more of them; I don't want to know them—I just know Hannah didn't come home until midnight. And she'd showered but I could still smell Blanche on her, still smell the lavender cologne.

And that was almost the end of us. Hannah slept in her pickup for several nights. Even Marge made a veiled remark about "the doghouse" when she saw Hannah's legs sticking out the passenger window of her pickup parked in my driveway. At least she had the sense not to go crawl back into bed with Blanche, though I bet that old sow offered. That would have been the last straw. No, Hannah was doing penance in that driveway and putting on a show.

I finally let her back in the house because I couldn't stand

the talk, people walking by my driveway and pointing out her feet sticking out her pickup window or her brushing her teeth in my birdbath.

But I wouldn't let Hannah back in my bedroom, wouldn't let her touch me, not even a hug for weeks. She knew she was being tested. Would she hop a freight or hop back on that curious old cow Blanche or would she stick it out with me? And would I stick it out with her? Well, you know the answer, but if this was *As the World Turns* they'd say, "Stay tuned."

Chapter Nine

HANNAH

Rachel'd been so glad to see me come home from World War Two, how could I be so dumb as to start World War Three right there in our own town? Oh, I knew I was in trouble. I'd always been careful not to take up with anybody local. I knew Rachel had her pride. But somehow, seeing that big ole Blanche looking so hopeful in her slip, I slipped. I'd known her all my life, but I never imagined I'd ever see her out of her corset. There she stood, pretty brave in her own way, and she said she'd always wondered what it would be like and now that her husband was gone she'd like to know.

Her bedroom was just off that hallway, too close for me to do the smart thing and change my mind. She pulled me in there by my belt, but once she got me in there I could tell she didn't really know what to do with me, so I thought maybe I'd just kiss her a little. Maybe she'd get cold feet.

But she liked it. Well, who wouldn't? I liked how that satiny slip felt when I stroked her breasts through it, big breasts, the kind that really fill your hands and your mouth when you start sucking a woman's neck and moving on top of her.

So there I was in my sweaty T-shirt, giving it to Blanche hard and deep. I do love to bury myself in a big-hipped woman from time to time. When she came she said, "Oh my" like she was surprised and then she kinda whimpered and barked, so I guess I was her first in a couple of ways.

I knew I should leave after that, but it didn't seem fair, so I explained the math of sixty-nine to her, and she was startled but willing. I'm all about education. And she did need to know what to do in case she got another opportunity. And she might. She confided there was another widow bowler in the Tuesday Night League who whispered to her once when she was drunk that she liked girls better.

I laughed and hugged ole Blanche and wished her good luck. And then, like a moron, I dropped off to sleep and woke up at midnight and knew I was in such trouble. Rachel would kill me—if I was lucky. If I was unlucky, she'd just throw me out and be all done with me. I'd rather die.

Blanche was still snoring when I left but at some point she'd left money in my shirt to pay for the patch job on her roof. That felt kinda funny, like a stud fee. But I guess if she'd paid for my labor with the sex that wouldn't have felt right either. Nothing about this was right and I knew it.

Rachel actually threw a kitchen chair at me. Yelled. Screamed. Cried. And pushed me out the door and locked it behind me. I could take all that, the chair, all the yelling, but it was the look in her eyes that made me want to drive off the dam.

How could I be so foolish? How could I risk everything like that to put another notch in my bedpost when all I cared about in the world was Rachel? And I knew the rules even if we'd never said them aloud.

So I waited her out—and I am no good at waiting. But I

waited. I threw my coat across me for a blanket and I slept in my truck in her driveway. I mowed her lawn and I washed up at the spigot at her back door. She says I brushed my teeth in her birdbath, and I wouldn't put it past me.

Finally, not because she'd forgiven me but because Rachel didn't like to hang her bedsheets out for the neighbors to see, she let me come inside and sleep on the sofabed her cranky old ma had lived on for a few years until she went to her glory (and mine).

I was indoors but still out in the cold, because Rachel wouldn't say a word to me. She cooked for both of us and we sat across the table eating, but she wouldn't say a word. And if I opened my mouth to talk, she gave me such a look that I snapped it shut and went back to chewing on her pork chops. I could barely swallow.

How long could this go on? Would it ever end? I'd hear Rachel's voice on the phone, talking to Marge or Karen Schneider and it just seemed so good to hear her voice. I knew I didn't deserve her forgiveness—I'd broken her trust diddling Blanche just two blocks away—but I swore over and over, silently, under my breath, to her cat Rhett Butler, with just my eyes, that I'd never do it again, not with anybody but her in the entire state of Michigan. Please, Rache, please.

She came home from church just livid all over again, because she'd spotted Blanche a few pews ahead of her just singing her lungs out on "Onward Christian Soldiers," Blanche sitting hip to hip to a milkman she was supposed to be keeping company with. There she sat, big as life, acting like nothing was wrong, like she hadn't just wrecked our life and was about to wreck his by leaving him for a bowler. Prob'ly it was all in Rachel's mind, but she thought Blanche looked especially satisfied with herself that Sunday, that even her clothes rode different on her big ole bountiful body.

Rachel said Blanche didn't meet her eyes on the church steps so maybe she was feeling guilty, but that wasn't enough for Rachel. She was boiling over mad at me all over again for

fucking a Methodist. And she wanted blood, preferably mine.

I was straddling a kitchen chair, kinda rocking on two legs, working on my checkbook and a pile of invoices and receipts when Rachel slammed in the back door and kicked the chair out from under me. I landed on my ass, which is where she wanted me. Fists on her hips, not looking a bit sorry, she hissed down at me, "I hope you're happy!"

Well, I was actually, because those were the first words she'd spoken to me in almost two weeks. I rubbed my tailbone and looked up at her, trying not to look too happy.

"Hannah Free, never again! You will never ever humiliate me in this town, this county, my church, my bed again. I don't care what you do when you're away—well, I do but not as much. I've learned to live with that. But I will not live with this. If you ever climb on some old cow I have to look at the rest of my life at church suppers and know you've been in a bed with her, or a car seat or a rowboat, I'm done with you. I will never be with you that way again. Ever. And I likely will murder you with my ax just so I won't be tempted. And no more pork chops either."

Suddenly I knew we were all right. She'd made a joke, two really, if you counted the part about murdering me. We were still a couple that jokes together. And she even helped me up off the floor.

But as far as our intimate life, she had to make the first move and it wasn't that day. Or that week. I stayed put on my sofabed. She grudgingly spoke a few more words to me each day. I finally fixed the transmission in her car. And we'd promised to take Barbara to the circus to see the elephant when the circus came to town, so we did.

Barbara was so little, she fell asleep before the lions came on, so I held her while Rachel ate pink cotton candy and watched the lions and clowns like she was the biggest kid there. Rachel'd never been to the Bronx Zoo like me or seen a brown bear in the wild, so she was pretty thrilled by that little one-ring circus, and she told Marge she should've come when

we delivered Barbara back home, still sleeping in my arms. But Marge had lost a baby the week before, so she just looked sad and kinda vulnerable and she and Rachel talked on the couch while I carried Barbara upstairs to her bed. Barbara started to wake up, so I sang her a little song. My voice would put anybody to sleep, and it worked like a charm. When I came downstairs, Rachel was holding Marge, and it looked like what both of them needed, so I went out to the car and waited till Rachel was ready to go.

Things were extra quiet when we got home, but late in the night I woke up and found she'd slipped under the blanket on my sofabed and had an arm around me. I was sleeping naked, always hopeful, so it was easy enough for her fingers to travel down my belly and slide inside. I knew she needed to take me first, so I rode her hand slow, getting reacquainted, and she did me just perfect, the way it can be when two people have been at each other as long as we had.

We were so good together. And I'd almost blown it. What a dope. What a lucky dope. I'd learned my lesson.

A few months later, I took off for Europe. There was money to be made in rebuilding all those bombed out towns—and it seemed like a decent thing to do. I saw myself as a one-woman Marshall Plan. Rachel packed me a lunch, but she went inside and didn't watch Dave's car pull out of her drive as he drove me down to Lansing to catch a bus. I wondered once if deep down Rachel'd like to see some sights with me, the Bronx Zoo, flamingoes in Florida, the Eiffel Tower, but she knew she had more pull over me staying.

I woke up, back in that damn nursing home, but if I shut my eyes for one more moment, I could see Rachel next to me in the half light of dawn that morning I left for Europe, her nightgown on the floor, me moving down, pulling her legs apart so one leg curled over my shoulder, listening to a sob catch in her throat as her hands tore at the covers, buried themselves

in my hair, just as lost in her want for me as I was in mine for her. I might have my way with a fraulein or a mademoiselle in Europe, but that'd be just to relieve the pressure. Rachel had all my feelings bundled up and locked away in her heart.

"Nice dream?" The kid looks at me from her chair and laughs. I bet I moaned in my sleep. I'd be embarrassed if I knew how to be.

"Yup. Pretty good dream." In my mind, I kiss Rachel one last time between her thighs then finally come up for air. I smile at the kid and stretch, listening to my bones crack—I'm a regular symphony in old age. "I'm surprised you're even up. We were up pretty late last night."

The kid leans forward, bangs in her eyes, and gives me that impish look. "Hannah, I'll have you know I've been up here for hours. I interviewed that old guy who was in here looking for his horses. He's pretty sharp when it comes to the Depression. He was in the CCCs, 'planted rows and rows of trees.' But he thinks we're still at war—the Big War. He asked me to save him a dance."

"Kiddo, you sure do know how to have a good time."

She laughs but then we both get kinda quiet for a minute. Turns out we're both thinking about Rachel, Rachel trapped in that room, prisoner to all that life-saving equipment that can't really give her back her life.

"Young lady, I'm real grateful to you for taking me to see Rachel." She reaches over to squeeze my hand but doesn't say anything. So I talk. "It's hard to see her like that. She'd hate it. Rachel was so strong, independent. She'd hate ending up like this, all wired up, just a body in a bed. Don't get me wrong, I loved being able to sit there and hold her hand, touch her face, her hair. That was good for me but it's no life for her."

The kid nods, quiet, in her own thoughts.

And in wanders Rachel's spirit, in a blue flowered dress I'd always loved, looking sleepy. She sees the kid's hand on mine, but she doesn't say anything, doesn't even look mad.

"I guess I'm not much better. We're both trapped in these beds. I used to just squander my energy. Hell, now I can't even tie a shoelace."

"But your mind's still okay."

Rachel chuckles. "I'd say that's up for debate."

I chuckle, too. "I like to think I've refined myself down to the essentials."

"So," the kid gives me a come hither look through her hair, "we going on vacation tonight?"

"You willing?"

"I asked."

I take her hand in both of mine and give it a tight squeeze. "Thanks."

"No problem." She stands, stretches, arches her back, getting ready to go.

"Wait. I wanna give you something."

"Just keep your clothes on, Hannah." As you might imagine, that came from Rachel.

The kid pauses on her way to the door. "You don't have to give me anything, Hannah."

"Yes, I do. And I finally thought of something you might like. Grab that old suitcase from under my bed, why don'tcha." I point, but it's easy enough to spot. It's an old suitcase smothered in travel stickers and (as Rachel would say) "Dirt from the four corners of the earth."

The kid shoots me a cute, puzzled look and leans down to tug the suitcase out from under the bed. Then she flops it down on her chair and, at my nod, flips open the latches and lifts the lid. Inside are a bunch of yellowed notebooks filled with my scribblings.

"My journals. The Depression's in there somewhere."

She's touching them all reverent like she's just stumbled onto the lesbo holy grail. "You really mean it, Hannah? You'd let me read them? I could quote from them? I'll try to skip over the personal stuff."

"Hell, if you can read my writing, you're welcome to it." I

79

slip her a grin. "Go ahead. You might learn something."

"I bet I will."

Rachel gives me the eyebrow. "I bet she will."

Snapping the suitcase shut, the kid picks it up and shoots me with her finger. "See you tonight. Three o'clock, kiddo."

I shoot her back. "It's a date."

And off she goes with every word I ever wrote, every thought I ever had. Even a novel. I hope after all this build-up, I'm not a disappointment. I watch her stride out the door then stop to say hi to a crumpled up old soul in a wheelchair then walk on out of sight. I miss her already.

Rachel's spirit is watching me watch the kid. Looks like she finally woke up because her nostrils are flaring. She shoots me with her own finger gun. "It's a date. Aren't you the nursing home Romeo."

"She is pretty cute—but not as gorgeous as you, toots."

That makes her smile, especially the "toots." But she's not backing down. "You old flirt. You never let me read those."

"You're in 'em."

"I hope you were kind."

"Not always." I'm being honest. I never was good at giving the answer that would keep me out of trouble.

Arms folded across her chest, Rachel is silently contemplating me like I am quite the crock of shit.

"They're journals, mostly. A few short stories. I had to be true to myself in my writing, Rachel. I couldn't sugarcoat it. The novel I wrote one year when I was snowed in—beat alcoholism." I wish she'd say something.

"Am I in that, too? Your novel?"

"I think you'd recognize yourself."

"So why did you give them to that young woman? Really?" She moves closer. I could touch her if only I could touch her.

Why did I give them to the kid? Rachel deserves an honest answer, so for once I'm sincere. "I guess I want to pass something on to somebody. I want somebody to know I was here."

"Well, I know." Rachel moves even closer. "We know."

"I want somebody to know you were here, too, honey. The real you, not the public you smiling at church bake sales. I want somebody to know about us who's not afraid to admit what 'us' means. I want somebody to know I took you to bed and I loved you."

Rachel gives me a tender look. "We know. That's what matters."

"But what about posterity?!"

The way that explodes out of me makes her laugh. I do love to make that woman laugh. "Posterity? Good Lord, what next?"

There's a swell, funny moment between us—and then it's over because in rolls the ancient horseman of the apocalypse, barging in on his walker like he owns the joint. He's damned surprised when he looks up from his feet and sees me.

I look right back at him. "Well?"

"Well what?" He plants his feet.

"What're you doing in here? Looking for your horses?" I'm pretty patient with him—I been having a good afternoon.

The old fart looks around, rattled. "Isn't this my room?"

"Nope." I shake my head and point. "You old guys are in the basement. Ask the nurse. He'll tell you where your room is."

Hoss isn't having such a good afternoon. He leans heavily on his walker. "I'm lost."

"I'll say you're lost. Go ask the nurse." I push the call button dangling from the railing on my bed.

The old guy's looking me over, squinting like he's trying to read a menu. "Do I know you?"

I start to give him a snappy reply, something smart-assed, but I stop myself and really look him over. "You know, bud, you do look a little familiar. I wish I could see a picture of you when you were younger." I try to picture him with hair, back straight, carrying a mailbag or fixing our television set. Or further back to that one-room schoolhouse ruled over by Miss Myrtle Duffield—could he be one of those boys I wrestled in

81

the dirt after school or whipped in a spelling bee?

He's squinting right back at me, prob'ly trying to picture me in a dress or fixing his TV. "What's your name? Who are you?"

I try to be funny. "Wanna take a guess?"

"No!"

"Then tell me who you are."

He chews his lip for a second or two, pondering. "How soon do you need to know?"

Rachel and I look at him with sad sympathy as Brad, the nurse, appears in the doorway. "Here you are."

The old guy looks at Brad. "I'm lost."

One of our nicer nurses and one of the only Blackledges not to land in prison, Brad gently but firmly takes the old coot's arm and gives me a smile and a shrug. "He never knows where his room is."

I look back at Brad. "He's looking for his real home."

The old cowpoke is still looking me over like I'm a rare spider in the cabbage salad. He narrows his eyes at me, frustrated. "I know you."

"Not anymore you don't." I say it kindly but it still hurts.

As Brad starts to guide the old fella out into the hall, the old guy looks over at Rachel's spirit then at me. "Your friend, she don't say much."

And off he goes, the only other barely living person who can see Rachel. She and I shake our heads at each other in amazement.

"Hannah. You should take a nap. Your little friend will be waking you up before you know it."

I give Rachel the eye. "I used to love to wake you up."

"By undoing my nightgown..."

"I'd be at your breast takin' a drink..."

"I hope that's not in those books you gave that girl to read."

"If it is, she'll enjoy it. Betcha anything she's like us."

Rachel rolls her eyes, long-suffering. "You and your 'gaydar.'"

Suddenly it's not so playful. "I never could convince you there was a whole world of us out there. And Rachel, you could never believe, not deep deep down, that what we did, who we were, was okay."

"Don't be silly." Rachel's pissed. Me too. We just never could leave a bone unchewed. "Didn't we sit on my porch holding hands, watching the sunset? Out there for all to see? Maybe not when we were thirty but when we were sixty."

"By then people just thought we were cute old ladies."

"Hannah, no one in this town has ever thought you were cute." Rachel plants her feet squarely and stares me down. "Everyone in this town knows what you are, Hannah, so they know about me too. But I shared my life with you in the town where I was born. I let go of all my privacy, because I loved you. Loved you staying right here. I never ran. I stayed home and let lifelong friends and family and nosy neighbors know just what I am. You show me somebody in one of your magazines from California who does that." Rachel's eyes are blazing. "Bunch of cowards. They say who they are, but they say it in San Francisco, preaching to the choir. I stood my ground, lived my life, and I loved you, loved you despite everything I was brought up to believe. So don't get on your soapbox with me, Hannah Free. Don't tell me anything."

And how could I? She was right.

We let a couple minutes go by in silence, simmering down. Eventually, after years together as a couple, you learn to say your piece but then shut up and calm down.

Eventually, I took a deep breath and made eye contact. "I'm tired."

"So am I." And I could see she was.

I cocked my head a little, voice husky and soft. "I wish we could take a nap together, Rache."

Eyes reaching deep into mine, she simply said, "I'll be there."

And she was.

Chapter Ten

MARGE

Knit one, purl two, knit one, purl two...

Mason won't wear the sweaters I've made for him. The man buys all his clothes at the Mt. Pleasant K-Mart, running like a deer when he hears there's a Blue Light Special on tube socks. Well, maybe not a deer.

Knit one, purl two...

I'm starting this sweater for Greta. Maybe she'll appreciate something handmade, appreciate the effort. If she'll even wear it coming from me.

I crocheted her a baby afghan when she was born—pink and white with seashells in the pattern. I mailed it to Barbara in Minneapolis. She sent me a polite thank you note like she was writing to a distant relative. Most daughters invite their mothers to help them after they have a baby, but Barbara had some hippie girlfriends help her birth Greta in a pond on campus. Lucky that little girl has a July birthday. I picture scads

of poor little hippie babies born in Minneapolis in wintertime dropping out and going skidding across an ice pond until somebody catches them.

Mama laughed and laughed when I told her that. Laughed and laughed. Hannah wasn't the only person who could get Mama to laugh. I haven't had much to laugh about in my life, but don't tell me I don't have a sense of humor.

"Remember, Mama, how we admired Greta's first baby picture?" I lean in and pat her hand, still and white on the sheet. "Greta was wearing the booties you sent and that little dress you made her." I remarked at the time how fortunate it was Barbara gave that poor little innocent baby a normal name like Greta. Half those little hippie babies ended up named Summer Solstice or Moon Glow. Mama claimed she liked both those names, especially Solstice; maybe she'd just call Greta *Solstice*. "You were just trying to get a rise out of me, weren't you, Mama? Tickled yourself so silly you got the hiccups."

I stand up and stretch and adjust the afghan on her bed, pet her arm through her nightgown sleeve. Then I sit back down. I do this dozens of times a day, otherwise my bad knee gets stiff. But I love to sit here with her. There's no place I'd rather be. Even like this, she's the best company I know. Plus I want to keep her safe. Hospitals and nursing homes are dangerous places. People need their families watching out for them.

I don't like her doctor, Dr. Baim. She's from Cleveland so she think she's hot stuff. Every time I see her she wants to have "a talk" with me. Well, we already had "a talk" months ago, and I haven't changed my mind one iota. Why is helping Mama breathe an "extraordinary measure"? Sometime we all need a little help. I'm pro-life like any good Christian person is, and that includes keeping Mama alive. I don't need that know-it-all woman from Cleveland to look all sad at me and tell me letting Mama go "would be for the best."

What would I do without her? She's always been my rock. Well, Jesus Christ is My True Rock, but Mama runs him a

close second. She'd be practically perfect if it wasn't for that darn Hannah.

I look over at the equipment breathing for her. "You hate this, don't you, Mama?" Mama liked to do for herself. Of course, when I lived to home, she had me do the dishes and share the ironing and in later years she turned over some of the holiday meals to me, though my Easter ham never tasted like hers. And Hannah kept the house painted and the roof tight and did help weed. And Hannah was good about mowing or paying Roy or a neighbor boy to do it when she was away. But it was Mama's house; she was in charge. Until this.

It's funny what can feel normal to a child. Hannah was away a lot. But her sometimes being there, sometimes not, just a colorful postcard in the mailbox, that seemed normal to me until other kids started telling me it wasn't, started telling me there wasn't anything normal about our situation. And I'd hear their mothers cluck to each other about what a scandal it was. Looking back, that was pretty mean, to say that loud enough for a child to hear.

Sometimes I wish I could've stayed four years old forever, never having to go to school, innocent as I was when I'd help Hannah plant Mama's tomato plants. Hannah and I would dance with the tomato plants, dance over the spot where she planned to plant them—she said dancing made the ground more fertile. She'd pick me up and swing me around like she was a ride at the county fair. I used to think Hannah was so much fun before I knew better.

Mama loved her though, loved her always, stood up for her, always let her back in the door, back in our lives. I know they had their fights, and I know Hannah hurt Mama's feelings taking off like she did, chasing around like a man, but Mama would sooner lose an arm than say a word against Hannah.

And I never did either, not in public anyway. If people tried to get something out of me, I'd never admit what I knew they were to each other. I'd just say Hannah was kinda weird but Mama and her'd been friends since they were children so

they were friends for life—that's just how Mama was, loyal as a bird dog.

I'm not so good about Mason. I let slip mean remarks over tea after Bible Study. I comment over how he's always napping, never talks to me. He drives a Schwan truck delivery route, selling pricey frozen goods to elderly shut-ins and harried singles and moms across two counties. He says by the time he gets home he's tired of making chitchat and just wants to sit in front of the TV and thaw out his hands after a day of digging potpies out of his refrigerated truck. I'd love a little chitchat.

"Mama, how can two people be married so many years and have so little to say to each other?" I stand up and flex my back and lean down to stroke Mama's cheek. "Did you and Hannah still have a lot to say to each other, even after all those years?" I know they did. And that really frosts me.

I sit back down. *Knit one, purl two.*

I close my eyes tight for a minute to rest them—after all these years of fancy work, I don't need to watch what my hands are doing. My mind wanders back to summer evenings watching the moonflowers open in the dusk. Hannah sent me the seeds from South America. They were just the most amazing flowers. They'd be tight in bud all day but as night was coming on, they'd start to bulge, and then suddenly, like fireworks, out they'd come. Hannah would set up lawn chairs and the three of us would sit and watch them open. We'd ooh and ah and applaud those strange, beautiful, night-blooming flowers. I don't understand to this day how they work. But watching them with Hannah and Mama that part never bothered me. That's a wonderful thing about being a child—magic just happens.

I hold the beginnings of Greta's sweater out for Mama to see even if she can't. She taught me everything I know about how to knit and crochet, how to cook and sew and remove stains. I'd wanted to make Greta's sweater with pink yarn, but I had a feeling she wasn't much for pink. I'd settled on a daffodil yellow, nice and bright. But I suppose whatever color

I go with will be wrong.

I reach over and pat Mama's hand. "Remember the moonflowers, Mama? I wish I had someone to enjoy them with me. I wish I had you back."

Chapter Eleven

HANNAH

Wonder why I'm dreamin' about moonflowers?

Those seeds I sent home from South America were one of the best gifts I ever came up with. The bongo craze lasted about a week—thank God—but those moonflowers bloomed beside Rachel's porch for years.

When Marge was little, we'd sit in lawn chairs and gape at those moonflowers. By the time they'd bloomed it was full night and Marge would be asleep in Rachel's arms. I'd take her and carry her up to her bed. Rachel would follow behind "buttoning up" the house, pulling shades, latching screen doors, swatting mosquitoes. Then she'd follow us up the stairs and kiss Marge and Roy goodnight.

Roy was too much of a boy for moonflowers. After a busy summer day being a boy on a bike, playing ball, terrorizing toads, he'd be asleep long before the rest of us.

arm. She smiles at the baby already nesting happily in my arms. "That's Marge. I think she likes you."

And I stood there and held that tiny baby for a full minute, Rachel's daughter, a marvel to behold. Baby Marge did take to me, cooing and drizzling like a leaky faucet. And big old palooka that I am, I didn't even drop her, which I sometimes regret.

So upstairs we went, the babies into a large crib together, me and Rachel into her big soft bed to make up for lost time.

I felt almost shy, kicking off my shoes and lying down next to Rachel in an actual bed, no hay or cows in sight. And since we'd last been together we'd both been with other people. But in the end all that fell away. We were the only two people in that bed. And despite how urgent I felt in the kitchen, once I was lying next to Rachel, I took my time. I nuzzled her ear, biting down lightly on the lobe. My mouth traveled down her throat and then back up to her mouth, and I held her in my arms and kissed her for a long time.

It was finally her who started unbuckling my belt and unzipping my drawers. She dipped her hands down in my pants and squeezed my rump as I put her underneath me and pulled her dress up over her head. She wrapped her legs around me and tore at the buttons on my flannel shirt—I didn't care; I knew she'd sew them back on.

I sucked her breasts through her slip and tasted milk. She laughed at the look on my face and pulled that milk-soaked slip over her head. "Don't worry. There's plenty." I rubbed my breasts against hers and kissed her eyes, her nose, her mouth some more while my hand tore off her underpants—I'd buy her another pair, something silky, maybe a whole bagful so I could keep tearing them off her.

She was already soaking the sheet underneath her. I ran my fingertips up the insides of her thighs, teasing her. She finally couldn't stand it anymore. In a voice deep in her throat, she said, "Oh *god*, Hannah, please."

Later, after she'd slipped away to check on the babies and feed them, later, after she'd dropped her robe and slipped back into bed with me, we'd talk for hours, laughing and cuddling and touching like it was the most natural thing in the world, like we'd never been apart.

Chapter Twelve

GRETA

Hannah and I have snuck off to visit Rachel several nights in a row. By dawn Hannah is exhausted, but when I ask if we're going again tonight she always perks up and says "Yeah, you bet."

After I settle her in next to Rachel's bed, I slip off to a chair in the corner and read Hannah's journals, so I'm respecting their privacy while at the same time invading it.

After I tuck Hannah back into her own bed, I'm still all wired up so I take off in my rental car and explore the geography of their lives, driving by old barns and chicken coops I bet they made love in under the kindly eyes of cows and chickens who chose not to pass judgment—okay, sounds goofy, but like I say I'm kinda wired up. And I'll bet cows aren't judgmental, but I'm not so sure about chickens.

I sit by the lake where Hannah's brother and Roy ice fished and Rachel rowed the shore looking for her husband's body floating in the lily pads. And Hannah skinny-dipped over there in the cove where there used to be no cottages. Of course, I grew up skinny dipping in frigid Minnesota lakes with my parents, so Hannah's not one up on me there.

If I was Hannah I probably wouldn't be in this car alone. I'd have picked up the night waitress just getting off work from the diner and I'd be sliding my hands up under her pink polyester uniform so I could go down on her just as the sun is rising. That's what I would do if I was Hannah. Instead, I'm scribbling a love letter to fax to Robyn from the motel.

I finish the letter sitting on the steps at Rachel's house. Somebody's keeping the grass mowed, but her gardens are grown up with weeds—she'd hate that so I set down my pages and spend an hour trying to pull up the worst offenders and carry them back to her mulch pile in a bushel basket I found by her back door. I'm glad to uncover all of her mums and black-eyed Susans, Rachel's old friends when Hannah was away.

I feel them here, Hannah and Rachel, playing checkers on the porch, watching the moonflowers, enjoying fresh doughnuts and cider in the fall as they took a break from raking. So many years, such a depth of loving that most of us only dream of.

Of course, I can also see Hannah slipping off at dawn in her fedora, carrying her suitcase, slipping away while she thinks Rachel is sleeping, but I'll bet she's not.

I broom away some cobwebs, because Rachel would want me to, then I go for pancakes at the diner.

I get a few looks, locals wondering who I am and why am I not just passing through. I wonder if Hannah got looks all her life or if people got used to her.

I know she and her brother Dave ate here a lot—she recommended the pancakes. I wonder which booth. I bet they always sat in the same booth.

She said lung cancer finally got Dave about ten years

ago—or it would have if he hadn't finished himself off in his garage with a handgun and a cigarette still burning between his fingers. Lung cancer's an ugly way to go, Hannah said. When he got the diagnosis, he shrugged, got his affairs in order, had a nice steak dinner then went out to the garage for that last smoke. He was considerate. Put a sign on the door saying, "Don't come in. Call the sheriff." Then Dave locked the door, sat down on a crate, smoked half a cigarette and pulled the trigger. Hannah spread his ashes in the Big Two-Hearted River. She teared up when she told me, but I know she kind of admires that Dave got to go out on "his own clock."

I picture Dave and Hannah and sometimes Hannah and Rachel in my booth as I finish every last bite of my pancakes.

I pull into the motel where I'm staying. Still seems funny to have so much money for rental cars and motels and grad school. For a couple of hippies who hated capitalism and thought the insurance companies were bloodsucking, greedy bastards, my folks had a crazy amount of life insurance—maybe Mom remembered hearing the story of Rachel rowing the lake after her husband's sudden death and had a practical moment when she was young and insurance was cheap. I'm not exactly enjoying the money, but I know Mom would be glad I'm spending a little of it helping Hannah and Rachel.

Something Marge said in her twenty-first birthday card to me clued me in she was abusing her power over those old women, thinking she knew best. I looked over at Robyn, who was grading papers across the table from me, and said, "I've got to go to Michigan."

Her forehead furrowed and she looked kind of concerned at me over her glasses. "Tonight?"

"No," I said, "but soon."

Speaking of Robyn, there's a fax from her at the desk at the motel. Very sweet—she misses me so I feel a lot better about not chasing tired waitresses in pink polyester. She's also over the moon about Hannah's novel and wants to get it published.

She's an editor at a small women's press and she's sure they'll do it, especially if she helps with the initial printing costs, which she says she'll be glad to do. I do love that woman.

I wonder if we'll be together for as many years as Hannah and Rachel. Robyn's older, but I seem to come from an accident-prone family, so maybe we'll come out about even.

I do want to have adventures, like Hannah. Maybe I should postpone grad school and train to be a long-haul trucker or work a summer on a Great Lakes fishing boat or travel to Peru and trek around Machu Pichu.

Or maybe I want to buy Rachel's house and spend summers here. Learn to patch the roof and bake cookies while Robyn does her research on the dining room table. Would Hannah and Rachel mind if we hung a rainbow flag from the porch and at the end of the day, I took Robyn's glasses and folded her book and pulled her up the stairs to Rachel's bedroom, to Hannah and Rachel's bed, and we carried on a fine family tradition? I bet they wouldn't mind.

Chapter Thirteen

HANNAH

Some new nurse, young with braces, Ashley or Olivia or something, wakes me up for some pills then again for a plate of mystery meat and potatoes. But all I wanna do is go back to sleep and dream of Rachel.

Do I ever dream about anybody else or dream nonsense about flying pigs—sure. But that's not what you wanna hear about. Me neither.

And since Rachel's spirit still won't come, I guess I'm going to have to dream in order to be with her.

So I dream cast about like I'm casting for fish. After a couple of false starts where I'm naked at the A&P and then I'm swimming upstream but not getting anywhere—yeah, yeah, Freud, I know—I'm lying on top of the covers in Rachel's bedroom. This is more like it. There she is, looking about sixty,

face with more creases but eyes still sharp. She's leaning over one of my shirts at her sewing machine. Lying there on her nice clean bed, I've got a screwdriver and a chunk of the lawn mower in my hands She gives me a look over her shoulder. "Why can't you work on that in the garage?"

I treat her to a toothy, winning smile. "But it's cold out there, Rache. And the light's better up here. Best of all, you're here."

"Oh baloney." But she laughs as she lines up my shirt and sews a few stitches.

I set aside what I'm working on and just watch her—it never gets old. "Rachel, why don't you put that away and come to bed. I can wear something else to Cousin Lily's funeral tomorrow. My bowling shirt's clean."

Rachel doesn't even deign to dignify that with an answer. She just snorts and goes back to her sewing. Bowling shirt. The very idea.

But I try again. I'm famous—or infamous—for my persistence. "Come on, Rachel. Nobody's going there to see me. They'll all be trying to look into Lily's casket to see what hair color they went with."

That makes Rachel laugh again, that throaty laugh I love. In life, Cousin Lily was as colorful as a petunia patch. Nice though. Not one to judge other people or make fun. Her own children came in a variety of skin tones long before it was fashionable, so she never gave us a hard time and neither did her kids. And Lily could hold her liquor, so she never got drunk and called me a carpet muncher or anything. And that was mild up to what some people called me. Oh well. I bet I'm a whole lot happier than they are.

Especially now, because Rachel's gotten up from her sewing machine and is walking toward the bed wearing what borders on a grin. She sits next to me and swings her knees up next to mine. She reaches for my hands and checks them, checks the nails. Pretty clean. Clean enough, I guess, because she holds onto them and leans toward me and I kiss her. Then

I sit back and just enjoy looking at her, every curve, every gray hair, every line in her face, even if she does say I put 'em there. Then I cross my arms across my chest, and I say, "Now you kiss me."

And she does.

And I get all cloudy-eyed and shake my head as I reach for her. "You are in such trouble." And my hand slides down to her breast and—well, you know the rest.

I wake up feeling better, relieved, less alone. Each to her own salvation.

Chapter Fourteen

MARGE

Mama's breath seems shallow, like she's fading. I ask the nurse to check on her, but after a couple of minutes Brad says nothing has changed, and he looks me right in the eye and says the machines will keep Mama breathing whether she wants to or not.

I give him a sharp look and he leaves but not before he shoots Mama a sympathetic nod of his head. Impertinent. If he thinks he knows so much, why isn't he a doctor? It's not his place to drop hints. And I don't want to hear them.

I sit back down next to Mama. "Men think they know everything, don't they, Mama?" My fingers are too stiff to do any knitting today—arthritis—so I go back to reading a magazine article about how to improve my love life. Now that's a lost cause. Mason only gets frisky after the Super Bowl.

But I've already read all the other articles so I might as well get a good laugh picturing me meeting Mason at the door wrapped in cellophane. Tomorrow I should bring a book. Or I could read Mama's Bible over there on her nightstand. Most days I can find comfort there.

I reach over to pat Mama's hand. I swear it feels a little cool. Mama's cared for several dying elderly relatives, hers and Hannah's, and she says when folks are leaving, their extremities start to cool off. But it doesn't seem like that should happen with these machines to keep her blood moving, to keep her alive.

Alive for what? Why? It's almost like Mama's standing over me, frowning, wanting to know why I won't just let her go.

I try to shake off the feeling and stand up to go, a little earlier than usual but I do need to grocery shop on my way home. "I guess I better go, Mama. Buy some pork chops. They're on special. Mine never turn out as good as yours but Mason is partial to them. And you know how he has to eat on time. If there's no pork chop in front of him at five thirty, he'll start slicing up the place mat, cutting it up into neat little squares."

I kiss her and stroke her hair before I go. But I don't tell her goodbye. It's not time yet. I just know it's not.

Chapter Fifteen

HANNAH

Just after I woke up, Nurse Cleo brought by her Boston bulldog puppy. What a wiggly, cute little guy; licked me up one side and down the other. It was nice of Cleo to put down her enema bag and drop by with the puppy on her day off. It's really a treat to see an animal, to pet a puppy up here. I miss being around cats and dogs, turtles, even all those cows, anything that doesn't smell of talcum powder and geezer piss.

The kid shows up a couple hours later wearing a baseball cap on backward and a really old Grateful Dead T-shirt. That T-shirt shoulda gotten a laugh out of me, but by then the puppy's worn off and I'm feeling glum. Some days seem longer than others up here, especially now that Rachel's spirit doesn't come. And nighttime, getting to sit with her, is a long way off. It'd help if I liked game shows.

The kid kisses me on the forehead and drops into the chair next to my bed. "So how they hanging, Hannah?"

"Smart-ass. I sure don't know what you're doing up here, kid. If I was your age you sure wouldn't catch me up here listening to some ole babe beat her chops."

"You weren't as sensitive as I am."

"Got that right." We laugh. She cheers me up. Nice having a friend.

"Hannah?" She's looking a little worried.

"Still here."

"I hope you won't be mad..."

"Well, whatever it is you can outrun me easy."

She's still looking a little worried—but also eager. "You know those notebooks you loaned me, your journals and the novel?"

"So what happened to 'em? Your dog eat 'em?"

"Hannah, they're wonderful!" She hops up out of her seat like she can't contain herself. "Wonderful! Especially the novel. I couldn't put it down. I thought you said the novel was no good."

"That's what I was told."

She's practically dancing. "It's set in Alaska, but it's you and Rachel, isn't it?"

I just nod. I changed a few details, but it's pretty obvious. So much for make-believe.

"I hope you won't mind, but I faxed it to a professor friend of mine. Robyn's an editor at one of the better women's presses. Hannah, she loved your book. She *loved* it. So I think they're going to publish it. I mean, it's not like it's some big publishing house in New York, but Hannah, people, other lesbians, will read your book."

Wow. "Jesus, that'd be great. I'd love to see that. Just tell 'em not to take too long at the printers."

"Hannah!" She slugs me none too gently in the shoulder. "Why didn't it get published years ago?"

I shrug. "I tried. Had a nice typed copy of it and sent it

out. A lot. And I got it back. Some guy at Random House or Scribner's sent it back with a real snotty letter. Said he was savin' me from 'further embarrassment.'"

"Why? Because your book doesn't have some man jacking off in a bull ring in Spain?"

"He claimed it was bad writing, but I s'pose the real problem was it's got two women together and neither one of 'em dies in the end. We didn't get to have happy endings in the Thirties." I shrug philosophically but back then, when I got that letter, I put my fist through a wall. "That was a long time before Beebo Brinker and *The Price of Salt*. I guess I was ahead of my time."

The kid's eyes well up. "But your novel is good. Didn't that count? How could that asshole do that to you?"

"Kiddo, critics ruin a career then go to lunch. What the hell. I still had quite a life. Had a great love. Traveled the world. Did exactly what I wanted to—pretty much."

"Except now."

"Hell, even now, it's not so bad coming to the end if you're not alone. If I could be sharing this room with Rachel, I'd be good to go."

"Shit." She starts to cry; half turns away.

I'm my usual sensitive self. "Well, don't blubber about it."

"You're awful." But I made her laugh.

I look her in the eye. "If I'm so awful, why do you keep coming back?"

She wipes her nose on a Kleenex from my nightstand then raises her head and gives me a defiant look through all those bangs. "The truth?"

"Always."

"Rachel really is my great-grandmother. I wasn't lying when I told the nurse that that first night."

"You're kidding." But she's not kidding. I can see that in her eyes. "But I met all her family."

"And you met me, Hannah. The last time you saw me I was seven. Grandma Marge didn't approve of my dad and mom

115

and how we lived our lives in Minneapolis. She got pretty ridiculous over Dad being a Buddhist. We stopped coming after that visit, but Great-Grandma Rachel would send me birthday cards with a five-dollar bill in them and she sent me comic books she said you picked out."

"Wonder Woman."

She grins. "So you really did pick them out."

I look her over, this petite little powerhouse in a Grateful Dead T-shirt she probably inherited from her father. I can see it in her eyes, that serious little girl in my old green rowboat concentrating so hard on trying to thread that night crawler onto a hook, giving me a big grin when that worm finally stayed put and she got to cast her line. "I took you fishing."

"To get me out of the house so I wouldn't hear them fight. I still remember you showing me how to bait my hook. And I remember Rachel's hot chocolate."

"Greta." Jesus Christ, I kept forgetting to ask her name, and she kept avoiding introducing herself. Greta. No wonder she seemed like family. "You wore that frilly pink dress."

"Well, not anymore. I'm just another flannel-shirt wearing Minnesota dyke. This editor friend that I mentioned, Robyn, is my lover."

"I thought you were one of the girls, all that talk about basketball and softball. But man, you sure didn't look like much of a baby dyke in that pink dress. I never woulda had you figured."

Greta laughs. "But I had you figured. You and Rachel."

I snort. "So am I your lesbian heritage? You gonna write a song about me and sing it in some lesbo coffeehouse?"

"Maybe." Greta's eyes twinkle like Rachel's when she's tickled.

"So how long you been out?"

"Officially? Since I started college. But I've always had crushes on girls. I dated a bunch of girls before Robyn—okay three—but she's The One. She helped me survive losing my parents. And underneath all that professor armor, she's pretty

shy, so I think I'm kind of good for her too."

"I just bet you are. A professor? Good for you. Raise the family up a notch. Don't settle for some rough-as-a-cob old-fashioned dyke like me or a frozen foods truck driver like your Grandpa Mason." My eyes narrow and I work up a good frown. "Holy shit, Jesus Christ, Marge is your grandmother."

"Sorry. That's why I wanted you to get to like me before I told you."

"Marge used to tell Rachel she was surprised your mom didn't name you Acid Flash or Summer Solstice." We laugh, but I'm remembering. "Your parents died when that drunk sideswiped them."

"Eventually they died." Greta braces herself. It's still awful to talk about. Hell, I can still puddle up about my mom and she's been gone for decades. Greta shivers despite the stifling air in the nursing home. "Dad died in the ambulance, but Mom was kind of like Rachel. Tubes and wires and machinery keeping her alive, if you could call it that. No brain function. I had power of attorney and their living will put me in charge if one of them died first and couldn't make the decision. So I had to decide about the equipment." She straightens up and looks me square in the eyes. "I let her go."

"I wish I could do that for Rachel." It's outa my mouth before I even realize I'm thinking it.

"Well, why don't you?" Greta looks around at my nursing home cell. "What could they do to you? Lock you up somewhere?"

She's sure got a point. "Yeah, it'd be a damn shame if I had to spend the rest of my life locked up somewhere."

"You must hate seeing her like that, trapped."

I know she's right. I can feel the waterworks ramping up and my voice catches in my throat. "I don't know if I've got the guts to say the last goodbye."

We both blink away tears. Talk some more. Finally we make a plan.

Chapter Sixteen

HANNAH

After some quiet time together, both lost in our own thoughts but keeping each other company, Greta takes off to catch some sleep at her motel and I drift in and out of sleep and dreams.

I'm a little kid again, running through a field of July corn. It's way over my head but I can hear Rachel, somewhere ahead of me, lost in the cornstalks. "Rachel?" I stretch out my hand, stretch and stretch, but I can't quite reach her, can't quite catch her or catch sight of her.

I wake up to take a pill then fade back into sleep and there she is! We're grown women dancing together to the radio in her living room. Rosemary Clooney is singing, "I'll be seeing you..." Rachel and I never got to dance in public, but I guess if I had to choose, I'd choose what we had, choose dancing with her alone over the bright lights of a disco.

My dreams fast forward to Rachel's bedroom. I'm reaching under the bed for my suitcase and there's a catch in my back because I'm sixty-two and used my back pretty hard over the years.

Suddenly Rachel turns up in the dream just like she did in real life. And she's not happy. "Hannah, what are you doing with that suitcase?"

"Suitcase? What suitcase?"

"The one you just shoved under the bed when you heard me coming. Where do you think you're going?"

I try to stand up straight and look her in the eye but I can't quite. "The Himalayas."

"Why?" She's got her fists pressed into her hips and is getting more pissed by the minute.

"I need a change. Mountains. Michigan hasn't got much in the way of mountains."

"Michigan has me." She's furious.

"You could come." Well, she could.

"Hannah, I am sixty-one years old."

"And you've never crossed the state line."

"I've never needed to." We're two graying old women in a bloody showdown that could end or save everything. "Hannah, what are you looking for?"

What am I looking for? I've never been able to explain my wanderlust to a hometown girl who loves her backyard better than anyplace in the world. So I just blunder on, throwing salt in old wounds. "New sights? Something different?"

"Different just for the sake of different?"

"Yes."

Rachel clenches her fists, trying not to wring my neck like an old chicken. "Well, that's the stupidest thing I've ever heard in my life, and I've been listening to you for over fifty years."

You know, sometimes I say exactly the right thing—and sometimes I say exactly the wrong thing. Like now. "Rachel, I'll be back."

"Don't you dare!" I swear I can see smoke and flames

pouring out Rachel's nostrils. Years of bottled-up anger comes flooding out in that bedroom with its ladylike lace curtains and late spring sunshine warming the old cat in the corner, who might just wake up if we get any louder. "If you walk out that door, Hannah Free, don't come back. Get your junk out of my garage. Don't send me any damn postcards. Go ahead. Go see your sights. Have a great time. But don't come back."

I feel like I'm caught up in a windstorm with no rope to grab onto, no friendly hand. I reach for her but she pulls angrily away. "Jesus, Rachel."

She's just about had it with me. I am the straw that broke the camel's back. "Don't you know where your home is? Don't you know that yet? Hannah, a dog is smarter than you. What do I have to do? What do I have to say?"

Being me I just throw the lit torch in the kerosene. "But what about what I want?"

"Hannah, all our lives have been about what you want. This is about what I want. You've had your chance to roam, now dammit stay home!" Rachel grasps my hands in both of hers and squeezes. "Stay with me. Sit on my porch with me and take me to the movies. Help me wash my windows and clean the cat box. Be here next to me in this bed all night, every night. Let me sleep a full eight hours and know you'll be here in the morning. Don't just visit, Hannah, live with me. Be with me."

I glance down at the end of my suitcase poking out from under the bed, at the stickers from Cairo and Peru and San Francisco. Then I look at Rachel, arms folded across her bosom, ready to love me to pieces or give me the heave-ho. "Rachel, I know every inch of this place, every nail, every flower, every bullfrog. There'll never be anything new to see."

"Stay." Her hands are on mine again but gentler this time. I can smell her lilac hand lotion, her VO-5 shampoo—not fair. "Hannah, if you can't find yourself, know yourself, *be* yourself here with me, where can you? Honey, it's not out there. It's here."

Oh, that smell of lilac. And the feel of her hands in mine. I nudge the suitcase under the bed with my foot and meet her eyes. "I'll try."

"You do better than try."

And I did. I think it surprised both of us.

The first few years I'd still take off for a few days at the end of a hard winter and drive until I found spring, usually in Kentucky, sometimes New Orleans. But then I'd drive straight home, usually breaking the speed limit because I was so eager to get home to Rachel and help her clean her cat box. As I grew older, usually a drive to Ludington or Harrisville to breathe in a Great Lake would tide me over one of my twitchy spells. Rachel would often go along on these drives with me. As I pulled in my boundaries she expanded hers. Besides, Ludington and Harrisville are both in Michigan so she didn't have to spoil her record for never crossing the state line. And every time, on the drive home, she'd gaze out the window all contented and say, all satisfied, what a beautiful state Michigan is.

And while we stayed at home, the world started to change. Drag queens in New York City kicked ass at a bar called Stonewall and put the police on the run.

I read about gay liberation and bought record albums in Ann Arbor with songs about women loving women (make that womym loving womyn). "Lavender Jane." Meg Christian and Cris Williamson. Gorgeous young dykes singing about their gym teachers. The best was not long ago buying a video of *Desert Hearts* and getting to watch it with Rachel. The book by Jane Rule was better, deeper, but you had to love all the sex and all the humor in the movie *and* neither of 'em died in the end.

After the movie was over we sat on the couch and talked it over for a while. Then we went upstairs to write another page in our own story.

Hard to believe it's finally time to end that story, but sitting here beside her, looking into Rachel's still face and all the "life support" equipment on the other side of the bed, I know it's time for all of us to just let her be.

Greta's looking both ways down the hall then comes back in. I'm not real worried about consequences. I know the nurses up here are real sensible about letting the hopeless cases slip away. Brad and I talked about it one night when he came by to check my vitals. Nobody knows better than a nursing home nurse why saying goodbye can be the kinder thing to do.

"Do it. Just do it." Wouldn't you know, Rachel's spirit has it in her to make one final appearance. I'm glad. She's sayin' what I need to hear.

I look over at Rachel's spirit then back down at flesh- and-blood Rachel. Her spirit is glowing with a last rush of life but fading at the same time. I wanna grab hold of both Rachels, young and old, and not let go. "Don't rush me, Rachel."

Greta's hanging back, trying to be discreet, so she doesn't hear what I said and thinks I said something to her. "What?"

"Rachel's here—I mean her spirit. And I'm still not doin' things quite the way she wants." I look back and forth between my two Rachels. I know I'm hesitating too long, and that's not our way. We were never ones to put things off. Wash the dishes right away. Don't let them sit till morning. And here I am, sitting and sitting, taking a hundred long last looks.

Quietly from Greta, "It's almost dawn, Hannah."

"Just a couple more minutes, okay? Let me sit with her just a couple more minutes." I hold Rachel's hand, which is cool to the touch. She's fading, I can feel it. Her life force is trying to go, but the machines chain her to the earth, breathing for her.

Greta is trying not to puddle up for my sake, but her eyes are shining. "We don't have to do it tonight, Hannah."

Spirit Rachel looks at me across a greater distance than just the room. "It's time."

I look at the Rachel in the bed. "Rachel, what am I gonna do without you?"

Greta gives in and starts to cry. "This is the kind of love I want."

"I hope you find it, kid. I'm just sorry you never got to know Rachel."

"But I do, Hannah. Through you."

Rachel's spirit smiles at Greta. "Goodbye, kiddo."

"Shit. Oh shit, I heard that." Greta sits down hard on a chair by the wall.

I look back down at my gray-haired old beauty in the bed. "So it's finally your turn to leave me, huh, Rachel?" I know I'm still stalling, but I can't help it. Rachel said I always had to have the last word. "Isn't it something how Greta turned out to be family, in more ways than one? Isn't it too bad we never got the chance to have Greta and Robyn come stay with us and eat your potato salad on the porch? Finally somebody to really visit with. Wouldn't we have liked that? Maybe I coulda even gotten you outa state to go visit them in Minneapolis for the gay pride parade." I chuckle picturing me and Rachel at the parade. Never in our wildest imaginings.

"Please." Rachel's spirit, faint but strong, urges me to get on with it.

I nod to her. "I know, Rachel, I know. That lawn's not gonna mow itself." I study the various plugs and switches. "Is this the right one? I don't wanna just disconnect the clock."

Rachel's spirit shakes her head and smiles a silent laugh. I can still make her laugh. I look over at her, my smile fading away. One last chance. "Are you sure this is what you want?"

She nods. "Hannah, I've had a full life—my God what a life—but it's over. Let it be over. Please, Hannah."

So I reach for the plug—

"What is going on here!"

I'll be goddamned if it isn't Marge. And I look her right in the eye and answer her. "Marge, I'm giving your mother back her life."

"Get away from her!" Marge grabs my wheelchair and tries to jerk me away from the bed, but I grab hold of the

railing on Rachel's bed and hold tight.

Greta jumps into the fracas and pushes Marge away from me. "Grandma, leave her alone! Hannah's just doing what you should have done months ago."

Marge turns on Greta, practically snarling. "Did you wheel her in here? How could you?"

"Hannah has a right to be here."

"She does not!"

They square off like two boxers about to trade blows. And Greta wades right in. "Of course, she does. They're lovers."

"I hate that word!" Marge actually covers her ears like she used to when she was a child and Roy would tease her.

"Grandma, I don't give a shit. That's what they are."

"You shut up."

"*You* shut up."

Marge clamps her arms across her chest, bristling with fury. "Greta, you don't know anything about this."

Greta stares at Marge in disbelief. "Of course, I do."

"Girls, stop it." I finally step in. "Marge, I'm glad you came."

"I'll just bet you are." Marge cries out like a wounded animal, because that's what she is.

Rachel's spirit murmurs, "It's time."

So I repeat it so Marge can hear. "It's time, Marge. You and me oughta do this together. This isn't about you. It isn't about me. It's about her. We both love her more than anybody. Saying goodbye to her hurts us more than anyone else on earth. But it's time."

A long silence. I can see the agony in Marge's eyes. She knows I'm right, but she can't stand to lose her mother, her favorite person in the world. "I can't."

I try to keep my voice calm, level, but it breaks a little. Marge hears it. Her eyes soften. The angry, hurt little girl in her is finally remembering who I am. I'm not the enemy. Marge can see I'm hurtin' just as bad as she is. "She's worn out. She's in pain. She's ready to go, Marge. We gotta let her go."

Marge looks at her mother, tears in her eyes. "I love her so much. And I've always been jealous of you, of how much you mean to her."

"Well, you kinda cramped my style sometimes, too, Margie, but I honestly did used to like you when you were a kid and I could get a smile out of you. We'd dance with those tomato plants."

Marge's eyes take on a distant look, a memory surfacing. "Remember watching the moonflowers? We'd sit and watch those moonflowers open like they were a fireworks display. I still have some in my garden, but nobody appreciates them like we used to."

"I would." Greta puts a gentle hand on Marge's arm, finally catching a glimpse of a grandma she might like to know.

Rachel's spirit grows more insistent. "Please."

And Marge hears her. "What was that?"

I nod to the still form in the bed. "Rachel."

"That's not possible." Marge backs away a step.

I keep my voice calm, firm. "Listen."

Rachel's spirit aims it directly at Marge. "Please."

"'Please.' Mom said, 'Please.'" Marge moves closer to the bed. She's crying.

So is Greta. "She wants you to help her, Grandma."

I sit up as straight as I can in this damned wheelchair and point. "Marge, how about you pull that plug. Greta, you turn off the IV. I'll turn this off. If anybody asks, if there's any trouble, I did it all. But I doubt they'll ask. It's time."

Marge, stricken but I can see she's coming around, touches her mother's hand. "Is this really what you want, Mama?"

Rachel's spirit answers, "Let me go, Marge."

Marge's face crumples. "But I'll be so alone."

"Get a dog."

I told you Rachel was funny, even at the damnedest times. I laugh.

Greta laughs.

Even Marge laughs. "Oh, Mama."

I pat Rachel's arm and look over at her fading spirit. "That's my girl."

Marge kisses Rachel's cheek. "I love you, Mama."

"Do you love me enough?"

Marge and Greta and me look at each other and down at Rachel. Finally, Marge nods.

"After we disconnect all this, we'll sit with her till she's gone. Marge, you hold her left hand. I'll hold her right."

As the machines quiet, I hold my girl's hand tight and I close my eyes and can see Rachel running across the autumn corn stubble, running away from me.

I open my eyes and see Rachel's spirit at the door, hanging up her apron. She gives me a last sweet smile. I whisper, "Wait for me."

And she's gone.

Hannah Free Extras

Behind-the-scenes interviews, impressions and thoughts on the making of *Hannah Free*, the movie.

Behind the Scenes of *Hannah Free*
by Tracy Baim, Executive Producer

Claudia Allen
Hannah Free Playwright and Screenwriter
by Jorjet Harper

Sharon Gless Takes Charge in *Hannah Free*
by Jorjet Harper

An Interview with Director Wendy Jo Carlton:
Hannah Free and the Mystery of Love
by Jorjet Harper

On The Set
Hannah Free Stars Talk about the Film
by Jorjet Harper

Sharon Gless
Hannah Free Q&A for Windy City Times September 16, 2009
by Richard Knight, Jr.

From Stage to Film
Laurie Attea on the set of *Hannah Free*
by Jorjet Harper

Sharon Zurek
Hannah Free Editor Extraordinaire
by Jorjet Harper

Perfect Pitch
Hannah Free Composer Martie Marro
by Jorjet Harper

Behind the Scenes of *Hannah Free*
by Tracy Baim, Executive Producer

Over the course of cinema's relatively short history, movies have profoundly shaped lesbian, gay, bi and trans culture, often in negative ways. Vito Russo documented the conflicted roles of LGBTs in cinema for his 1981 book *The Celluloid Closet*, which was made into a documentary after he died. By the time the film came out in 1995, there was a new day dawning on the film landscape, with many more positive portrayals inside and outside of Hollywood, largely due to the growing strength of the LGBT community.

As a journalist covering the LGBT community since 1984, in the era of *Desert Hearts* and *Personal Best*, I have witnessed firsthand the powerful way these movies reflected our lives. We as a community may not always love every depiction of ourselves on the big or small screen but we can acknowledge that our community, and sometimes society, is changed each time another aspect of our lives is shown onscreen. Sometimes the impact is mostly within our community, but increasingly that impact has helped shape our movement in the mainstream by educating our allies and our own younger activists, with films such as *Milk* or *Brokeback Mountain*, or TV shows including *Ellen* or *Queer Eye for the Straight Guy*.

As a journalist and newspaper publisher, I believe in the important role LGBT media has played in covering and shaping our movement. But I have always been drawn to the more permanent format of film. In the early 2000s I started to work on a potential film, *Half Life*, based on a story I had written about lesbians in the military. It was adapted for the stage, but by late 2007, it was clear the timing of doing a military film was too risky, so I decided to focus my energy on launching The Chicago Gay History Project, an oral history shot on high-definition video, now online at www.ChicagoGayHistory.org.

In December 2007, I was invited by gay playwright Nick

Patricca to a Victory Gardens theater production. There I ran into Claudia Allen. Claudia is among the most prolific and produced living lesbian playwrights. She is a native of Michigan, and the primary home for her work has been Chicago, where she is a playwright in residence at Victory Gardens. Her plays have been produced around the U.S., but none had yet made it to the lasting format of film. I wanted to interview her for the History Project, so we made a plan for a video shoot while she was in town that week.

I picked Claudia up and drove her to the interview, and during the ride we discussed her work. I still wanted to do a movie, and when I brought up the subject of translating her plays to film, Claudia said that she had been approached in the past and it had never felt right, but that she would trust me with her stories. Wendy Jo Carlton, who had been shooting my history videos, had directed several short films, so the three of us discussed it briefly at the gay history interview and felt it might be fate to try and pull off a full feature film: for all of us, it would be our first. Claudia would write the screenplay, Wendy Jo would direct, and I would be executive producer (a fancy title for raising money and paying bills).

I suggested *Hannah Free* among all of Claudia's plays because I had seen it twice, and loved it, and also because I knew how few films had addressed the issues of aging in our community. As a fan of the film *Fried Green Tomatoes*, I also yearned for a film that showed previous generations of lesbians actually kissing and being intimate.

The three of us met again a few weeks later to begin our formal commitment to the making of the film of *Hannah Free*. Claudia worked hard on adapting the script to become a more cinematic story, with advice from Wendy Jo. I created a business plan and founded Ripe Fruit Films as an Illinois corporation. In the summer of 2008, we hired Chicago filmmaker Leigh Jones to do a preliminary budget, and set about the task of raising money and enlisting crew through various Chicago connections. Musician and Web designer Martie Marro came on board that summer

to start discussions about music, sound and the launching of our Web site. Thus we became four lesbians in search of a film.

Our timing would be tricky, and was primarily based on the main ingredient: Sharon Gless, star of such TV shows as *Cagney & Lacey, Queer as Folk, Burn Notice* and *Nip/Tuck*. Gless had been a friend of Claudia's since they worked together in the 1990s. In the spring of 2008, Gless agreed to take on the film's starring role. She was shooting *Burn Notice* for USA Network that summer and into the early fall, and there was a threatened industry-wide actors' strike. We realized that we would have only a one-month window of opportunity to have Sharon in Chicago: November 2008. So all of our fundraising, crew and casting were timed around this.

In early September, we held two weeks of auditions. L.M. Attea, who had directed the first staging of *Hannah Free*, in 1992 for Chicago's Bailiwick Theatre, ran our casting weekends. We really lucked out with some amazing Chicago-based actors. Taylor Miller of the soap opera *All My Children* was signed as Marge, Kelli Strickland as the young Hannah, and Maureen Gallagher and Ann Hagemann as older and younger Rachel. Two bright young girls, Casey Tutton and Elita Ernsteen, signed as the very young Hannah and Rachel. Jacqui Jackson, just out of DePaul University, signed on as Greta. And some great character actors filled out the other roles: Meg Thalken, Patricia Kane, Elaine Carlson, Les Henderyckx, Bev Spangler, Shawn Murray and more. Some of these seasoned actors from Chicago theater had been in various stage productions of Claudia's, including *Hannah Free* at Victory Gardens.

As October neared, the U.S. economic crisis and presidential election loomed large over our fundraising. Several of our investors lost huge amounts in the stock market, but they remained committed to the project and its importance for our community. Our investors were diverse: gay and straight, male and female, young and older, mostly from Chicago but also from around the country. We had already started our train in motion, with crew and cast coming to town, so we were "all in" by mid-

October. Director of Photography Gretchen Warthen and her team began shooting on November 3.

By this time, we had already almost doubled our budget (and by the end of post-production it had tripled), but we were fortunate to have a lot of contributions, small and large, of both cash and needed supplies and food. We also signed on new investors, and held a great fundraiser with the cast during the film shoot, at the Center on Halsted in Chicago. Later, we also held house parties across the U.S.

The filming starts

Hannah Free was shot in 18 days: 17 days in the home my sister and I live in on Chicago's South Side, and one day on location in south suburban Beecher, Illinois, at the wonderful home and farm of Joyce and Ray Horath. During our three-week shoot, hundreds of people participated, from those donating their old cars for a period scene, to carpenters, painters, lawyers, production assistants and beyond.

Sharon Gless had agreed to stay in the coach house of our 1870s home, so it was convenient for her to go back and forth from the main sets to her residence in between scenes. Claudia Allen stayed in the same coach house, and other out-of-town crew stayed in the front house or in neighboring homes. Even the next-door neighbors were helpful, allowing lights to be staged from their window, and one property owner let us use his large lot for parking. The city park next door doubled as nursing home grounds, and an alley cat helped "direct" our shooting in that location. (We named her Joy, for my late mother, and a production assistant adopted her. We told straight crew members that while a black cat may normally bring bad luck, on a lesbian film set it was good luck; plus, our editor's company is named Black Cat Productions, so you can't beat that for a good omen.)

The nursing home itself was also named for my mom, The J. Darrow Home, since the mansion had been hers and our late stepfather Steve Pratt's. Our "Spirit Rachel" actor and others felt

the presence of Mom during the shoot. My family was all in on the act, with sister Marcy serving as location supervisor, her then 11-year-old son Anthony allowing his room to be used for light staging, and my dad Hal Baim shooting more than 20,000 behind-the-scenes photos. My cousin Megan Drilling, an architect, designed the sets, with the amazing Rick Paul as our production designer. Rick found every kind of prop needed, along with his team, including Assistant Art Director Beth Gatza. Iris Bainum-Houle was our fantastic wardrobe designer, with Jillian Erickson and Budd Bird handling the complicated makeup and hair.

We transformed the 1870s mansion into 17 sets from several decades: the nursing home, a women's army barracks, a 1940s New Mexico café, living rooms, bedrooms, an Alaskan fishing shed, a kitchen, hallways, a nursing station and more. Our makeup, hair and wardrobe people worked at a frantic pace, as did sound and lights. We worked against the clock, the weather, and noise from construction crews, ambulances, kids playing in the park and creaky floors and plumbing of the old mansion. The day we shot scenes on the farm, the temperature for outdoor scenes was freezing, and rain and snow threatened the entire time.

At our main location, the rain was sometimes so bad that the backyard turned into a mud pit. Sharon Gless was concerned about those having to walk back and forth in this mud, so she asked production assistant David Strzepek to drive her to Home Depot, where they purchased a dozen large wood pallets, and brought them back to place them as a bridge over the mud. It was my favorite day on the set—our warm and generous star Sharon pulled up mud-encrusted, half-submerged cardboard sheets that had been our makeshift solution, and helped put down the much more sturdy, serviceable wood planks. We kept telling Sharon that we could finish it, but she insisted on getting down and dirty with the crew—and it was her one day off that week!

This being my first film set, I was never quite sure what was normal and what was not. There were strong differences in interpersonal styles based on gender, age and sexual orientation. Our crew and cast were of all ages and sexualities, and sometimes

that made for a fun set, and sometimes it created communication difficulties. But from what I hear from the more experienced crew, it was actually a dream compared to many other sets. Good food helped bridge some gaps: Ann Sather Restaurant donated hot breakfasts every morning, which my partner Jean Albright picked up, and Amy Bloom and Sharon Brown coordinated hot meals for lunch every day.

Our production team included Unit Production Manager Shadie Elnashai and Production Coordinator Don Ferguson; our first assistant director was Ed Koziarski and second assistant director was L.M. Attea. Blair Scheller ran the sound mixing, with sound supervisor (and later music composer) Martie Marro and their team. Gaffer Clifton Radford and his crew coordinated the lights, which were a challenge in the small environment— the old mansion needed major plaster repairs and painting after the shoot was over. The production assistants included Cynthia Appleby, the Key PA who was on set every morning by six a.m., plus PAs on the set almost every day such as Brad Deron, and then volunteers who were only able to come one or two days on set. The PAs were all amazing and a great support. We had a terrific editing team working after hours downloading files: Justine Gendron and Sarah Plano, reporting to our editor Sharon Zurek, burned the midnight oil as the rest of the house slept.

We began our shoot the day before the historic Nov. 4, 2008 presidential election, so most people had voted by absentee ballot, including Sharon Gless, who lives in Florida. The energy was high that Election Day Tuesday, and we broke shooting a bit early so folks could attend election parties—including one that Sharon was hosting in her coach house residence. Out-of-town Barack Obama workers actually were living on the third floor of the main house during the shoot, but we rarely saw them, unless we had to stop action on the set to let them in or out.

The party was getting started in the coach house, as well as one mile north in Grant Park where the Obamas would later appear. But then a crisis struck—one of Sharon's contact lenses would not come out. Our contact lens advisor, Cason Moore, was

Writer Claudia Allen on the first day of shooting for the film *Hannah Free*.

Ann Hagemann (younger Rachel) and Sharon Gless (as Hannah).

The South Side Chicago home where 17 of the 18 days of filming took place.

Director Wendy Jo Carlton on the first day of shooting.

The nursing home in the film, The J. Darrow Home, was named for the mother of executive producer Tracy Baim and her sister, site location supervisor Marcy Baim. Joy Darrow died in 1996.

Jacqui Jackson (Greta) on the set with the good-luck black alley cat that joined the set on the first day. She was adopted by crew member Sharon Brown and named Joy Virginia.

Executive Producer Tracy Baim and Music Composer/Sound Supervisor Martie Marro.

Actor Jacqui Jackson (Greta).

Director Wendy Jo Carlton with Production Designer Rick Paul and Art Director Megan Drilling.

Extras actor and production assistant David Strzepek with Director Wendy Jo Carlton.

Director of Photography Gretchen Warthen.

Maureen Gallagher (older Rachel).

Assistant Art Director and Set Decorator Beth Gatza.

Maureen Gallagher and Sharon Gless get ready for a scene in *Hannah Free*.

The actors with Director Carlton.

In these photos, Kelli Strickland (younger Hannah) and Ann Hagemann (younger Rachel) show the passion of their characters.

145

Second Assistant Director Laurie Attea, who was also Casting Director.

Sound Utility Katie Jacobson and Key Production Assistant Cynthia Appleby.

In these two photos, Patricia Kane plays the Minister opposite Sharon Gless as Hannah.

Director Wendy Jo Carlton with Rick Paul and Tracy Baim (top) and
Script Supervisor Kristin Owings (below).

Meg Thalken (right) plays the Mail Lady opposite Sharon Gless.

Gless with Ann Hagemann as Spirit Rachel.

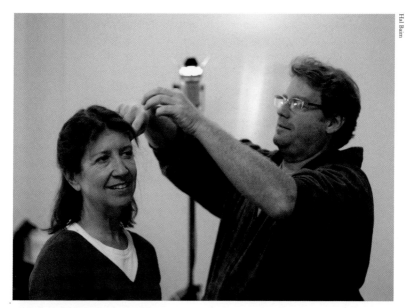

Hair Designer Budd Bird with Maureen Gallagher (Rachel).

Make-up Designer Jillian Erickson with Elaine Carlson (Day Nurse).

Hair Designer Budd Bird with Taylor Miller (Marge).

Sharon Gless in both photos opposite Maureen Gallagher.

Costume Designer Iris Bainum-Houle had to dress actors across multiple generations.

On set in Chicago, from left: First Assistant Director Ed Koziarski, Director of Photography Gretchen Warthen, Director Wendy Jo Carlton, and actors Jacqui Jackson and Sharon Gless.

Kelli Strickland plays younger Hannah. Top left are hats from the film tagged with production tracking.

Kelli Strickland and Ann Hagemann in one of the movie's sexy flashback sequences.

Jacqui Jackson (Greta) visits Sharon Gless (Hannah).

155

The youngest Hannah and Rachel characters are played by Casey Tutton
(Hannah) and Elita Ernsteen (Rachel).

Director of Photography Gretchen Warthen.

Quinn McCauley Coleman and Daniel Justus Rock-Hughes play the babies Marge and Roy. The real-life parents of each child are lesbians, and the moms were on set for filming.

Kelli Strickland (Hannah) and Ann Hagemann (Rachel) with Meredith Drilling-Coren (daughter in real life of the film's Art Director, Megan Drilling) as young Marge.

158

Director Wendy Jo Carlton with Director of Photography Gretchen Warthen.

Maureen Gallagher and Sharon Gless.

Kelli Strickland and Ann Hagemann.

Maureen Gallagher and Sharon Gless.

Jacqui Jackson and Taylor Miller.

Taylor Miller out of costume and out of the hair --- which was actually her own hair teased up by Hair Designer Budd Bird.

Writer Claudia Allen with Sharon Gless.

The film's editor Sharon Zurek (middle) with her assistants Justine Gendron and Sara Plano on set.

Maureen Gallagher and Sharon Gless.

The three generations of Hannahs and Rachels posed for a photo on the one day all were on set together, the shoot on the Beecher, Illinois property donated by Joyce and Ray Horath. From left: The Hannahs (Casey Tutton, Kelli Strickland and Sharon Gless) and the Rachels (Maureen Gallagher, Ann Hagemann and Elita Ernsteen).

Celebrating at the cast and crew wrap party at Polo Cafe in Bridgeport, Chicago. Back row from left: Ann Hagemann, Wendy Jo Carlton, Claudia Allen, Kelli Strickland, Sharon Gless, Jacqui Jackson and Maureen Gallagher. Front: Bev Spangler (Night Nurse), Elaine Carlson (Day Nurse), Meredith Drilling-Coren and Tracy Baim.

At the world premiere of the film, at Frameline in San Francisco, June 28, 2009 on Pride Sunday, on the 40th anniversary of the Stonewall Riots in New York that started the modern gay and lesbian rights movement. From left: David Strzepek, Gretchen Warthen, Claudia Allen, Martie Marro, Tracy Baim, Sharon Zurek, Wendy Jo Carlton.

Sharon Gless and Rosie O'Donnell, who introduced the world premiere of *Hannah Free* June 28, 2009 in San Francisco. The film, screening as the Closing Night Frameline film at the Castro Theatre, sold out several weeks ahead of time.

Actors Jacqui Jackson and Maureen Gallagher autograph covers of the book version of *Hannah Free*, from Bella Books.

Taylor Miller, Sharon Gless and Claudia Allen in San Francisco at a special cast and crew party at Orson restaurant the night before the film debuted.

Kelli Strickland and Martie Marro at the post- screening party.
At right: Tracy Baim with editor Karin Kallmaker on opening night.

Writer Claudia Allen with Karin Kallmaker in San Francisco.

Sharon Gless on the set of *Hannah Free.*

The cast and crew gather for a photo at the Sept. 26, 2009 Chicago premiere of *Hannah Free,* at the sold-out Gene Siskel Film Center.

called, and he kindly diverted his cab full of groceries and a friend to come to our house. Even he couldn't remove the lens, though, so he called his boss at a downtown hospital, and I drove Sharon to the hospital just as Obama's victory celebration was beginning to clog the streets with jubilant people. We avoided the closed streets for the rally. Sharon, ever the trooper, ran dialogue with her assistant Kate Mahoney as we waited for the eye doctor to arrive. All was well when the calm doctor did his work.

By the time we returned home, victory was clear and Obama was speaking to the nation. There were also mixed emotions as it became clear that the anti-gay marriage Prop 8 was passing in California, as was a similar ban in Florida. I myself was emotionally exhausted from the hospital drama, worried for Sharon's health and the film. She took it in stride and was ready for her seven a.m. call the next day. Sharon and all the actors were so friendly around the set that by the time of the wrap party, held at Polo Café on the Southwest Side, everyone was excited to celebrate together. At that event Sharon stood for more than two hours, posing for photos and signing autographs. We could not have had a better, more gracious leading lady.

What are the ingredients of making a movie? Well, you first start with a script, then add in great actors and crew. But truly, what you also need is something more mystical and magical, something you can't plan for or hire out. With *Hannah Free*, we experienced a series of little miracles, and were fortunate enough to have a little magic mixed in. It may have begun with Joy, the black cat that first day on the set, as she assisted the team walking through the park. Who knows? One thing I learned for sure is that no amount of training or planning can prepare you for all the ups and downs, the exhaustion, personalities, quirks, and quirks of fate that await you on a film set.

Post-production: The real fun begins

The build-up and actual shooting of a film, as exhausting as it can be, is really just the beginning. After we wrapped in November

2008, director Wendy Jo Carlton, music composer Martie Marro and editor/post-production supervisor Sharon Zurek began their intense collaborative work. Katie Jacobson, Anne Hanson and Laurie Little assisted with creating a sensational trailer to tell, in two minutes, the story of *Hannah Free*. We used that trailer for several months of additional fundraising, visibility and buzz-raising.

While I worked on film festivals and other fundraising and distribution issues, the critical work of finishing the film was in the hands of Wendy Jo, Martie and Sharon. Claudia Allen and I also continued to raise funds, and we had some great last-minute investors come through to help our post-production costs such as sound mixing and colorizing at two terrific Chicago companies, Resolution Digital Studios and Nolo Digital Film. Director of photography Gretchen Warthen returned to town in April to do some b-roll exterior staging shots with Wendy Jo, using the same gorgeous high-definition digital video camera as we had used on the shoot.

Starting in March 2009, we hosted house parties across Chicago and the U.S., with the final one on May 1 in Seattle. Party hosts screened the trailer, gave away prizes and raised critical finishing funds. While the fundraising was important and necessary, we also began to apply to film festivals.

We had decided we wanted our World Premiere at the oldest and most prestigious LGBT film festival, Frameline in San Francisco. Frameline is held in conjunction with LGBT Pride, so we were fortunate to get the coveted Closing Night film slot, June 28, 2009, at the 1600-seat Castro Theatre. To add to our excitement, this coincided with Pride Sunday, and was also the 40th anniversary of New York's Stonewall Riots—the start of the modern LGBT-rights movement. Most of the cast and crew were there, including Sharon Gless, and the film was introduced by Rosie O'Donnell.

One of the things I learned in my crash course on film is that a lot of independent filmmakers get stuck in this final phase. They run out of energy and funding, and take the first good deal

they get. But independent film has entered a new age, partly due to the digital transformation, which has caused a distribution transformation. It's no longer all about theatrical showings or even just festivals. It's also about video on demand, DVD, TV and a multitude of ways to get a film in front of an audience. The goal, of course, is to get the film out to as many viewers, worldwide, as we can reach.

To further expand the reach of this important story, Claudia Allen has written this novel for Bella Books. We may also produce a soundtrack of music inspired by the film. Additionally, we have a Web site, www.hannahfree.com, both a Facebook group, Hannah Free film, and a Facebook Page for fans, Hannah Free. And we have a Twitter account, HannahFree. Whatever new ways we can utilize to reach an audience, we will be there.

If you want a wider range of choices when it comes to film, supporting independent cinema is a major way to make that happen. By viewing and buying lesbian movies, you are part of a long and important support network that makes future films more possible. And through film, we in some small ways do change the world. As Claudia Allen likes to add to her autographs these days: "Hannah Free ... free at last"—free to help show the world the truth about the challenges many older lesbians and gays encounter.

was having. Nobody was writing for women in those days. No one had the material except us. I think the show was a hit because these two women talked about their feelings. On television, two heroes didn't talk about their feelings—they just went and solved crimes or they performed surgery or they went to trial. There wouldn't have been an *NYPD Blue*, where men talked about their feelings. On *Cagney & Lacey*, feelings were discussed; we were the first to do it."

With two women stars, *Cagney & Lacey* had a huge fan base among lesbians. Both detectives were written as heterosexual, but at a time when there were no out lesbian characters on television at all, lesbian viewers could watch *Cagney & Lacey* and revel in any subtext that might hint, no matter how slightly, of hoyay. "The lesbian following was quite extraordinary," says Gless. "Judging from the mail, it was Cagney's character that attracted the lesbian audience, and I'm so grateful. The gay community has kept me going, all my career, since then. But I think a lot of people didn't believe that Cagney wasn't in love with Lacey. There were fantasies about us, and everyone thought that Christine really was gay. They thought I was gay. And I think it was the strength of Cagney: she was single, she was feisty, never stayed with one man. I think—and I say this with great modesty because I didn't write it—I think Cagney is still the best, most complicated woman ever written for television. She was troubled, she had attitude and she was boyish. I insisted that all my jackets come from men's stores. It wasn't intentional to attract the gay and lesbian audience, it just did. And I enjoyed that, it was fun for me. But it wasn't planned that way."

Queer as Folk

After seven years of *Cagney & Lacey*, and several more on *The Trials of Rosie O'Neil*, Gless found that the choice TV offers had dwindled. "I started doing theatre. I hit fifty years old, I went into menopause, I quit smoking, and put on sixty pounds. So nobody was really interested in hiring me." One of the stage plays Gless

did was in Chicago at Victory Gardens, in Claudia Allen's *Cahoots*. She also met drama coach and agent Peter Forster, who "called me up and said, 'You're perfect for this part, let me send it to you.' I said okay. Well, I flipped." It was the part of Debbie Novotny in *Queer As Folk*. "It was so daring I knew it was going to be trouble, and I love trouble. So I called Showtime and said I wanted the part. The head of Showtime said he liked that idea, that it would bring a little class to the project. I said, 'Tell him class is not what I had in mind!' I asked the producers, before I went out to meet them: 'Do you know what I look like?' because I was heavy, and they said, 'Yes we do' and they wanted this. So I got the job." And as a result, Gless's career again went into high gear.

"On *Cagney & Lacey* I learned about feminism," says Gless. "Then I went to do *Queer As Folk*. I thought I knew everything. All my best friends were gay. Sounds like a cliché, but it was always more fun hanging out with gays and lesbians, it was just more fun. But I learned so much on that show too, and it again was groundbreaking. How many times does lightning strike twice in a career, with truly groundbreaking shows? And I was just lucky enough to play them both. It changed my life. And since *Queer As Folk*, I haven't stopped working."

Loving Hannah

Respect for the work of Claudia Allen was the main reason for Gless's participation in *Hannah Free*. "I've had the great pleasure of doing Claudia Allen's work in three different forms," Gless recalled during filming. "In 1994, Tyne Daly and I did *Deed of Trust* for radio here in Chicago. Then in 2000, Claudia invited me to come do *Cahoots* on stage. And now here I am doing *Hannah Free* on film. The reason I was excited about doing it is that Claudia wrote it, and she writes women beautifully. And she's very funny. And she makes me cry. She does all those things that I want to do for people when I play a role, built in when it's one of her projects."

"I love Hannah," says Gless. "She isn't anything like Christine

181

Cagney but she's got the same feistiness, the same independence and a little immaturity. She's a tough one, but there's a sadness to her that appeals to me. I love that she traveled all over the world, but she'd always come home to Rachel. I love the fight in her—and that's really what this story is about. It's about the whole lifetime of these women, from the time they're ten years old, but the thrust of it is Hannah's fight to get into the room to be able to say goodbye to the love of her life. And the daughter won't let her in."

One of the characters the elderly Hannah speaks with often during the play is the spirit of her lover Rachel, who lies in a coma in another wing of the facility Hannah lives in. "I happen to believe there is an afterlife, that the heart does go on, and the people who've preceded us in death are with us—the veil is that thin. So the character of Spirit Rachel was right up my alley."

Since Hannah and Rachel are depicted from the time they were children on into old age, several different actresses played the parts. "The younger Rachels and Hannahs have a lot of sex," says Gless. "The older ones don't. But there was one scene where we were supposed to snuggle and tenderly kiss." To prepare for this scene, Gless and Maureen Gallagher, the actress who played Hannah's lover Rachel as an older woman, went to dinner. "I took her out to a very nice Chinese restaurant," recalls Gless, "and we just sat and talked about our personal lives. I just thought it was important that we get to know each other, especially if I was going to have my tongue in her mouth."

Gless thought it was important to perform the final scene of the movie with spontaneous feeling despite numerous takes. "In a scene like that, I try not to plan what's going to happen. I don't have a technique. I kind of fly by the seat of my pants, and sometimes there are tears there and sometimes there's not. I had a coach tell me once, 'Sharon, it's not important that you cry, meaning me—it's important that they cry.' So sometimes the scenes would come up tears, but I never knew from take to take what was going to happen. As long as I kept it honest, that's the most important thing, that honesty. But I wanted the audience to

feel the loss Hannah was feeling."

Gless points to *Hannah Free*'s relevance to the issue of Proposition 8, forbidding gay marriage, but adds, "Claudia wrote this years and years ago, before any of this was an issue on the political forefront. It's amazing that, tragically, Proposition 8 passed in three states while we were shooting *Hannah Free*, which is a little piece of that story. But it's more than that, too; it's a love story. And I do believe love wins."

Gless remains a featured actress in *Burn Notice*, which has been renewed for a fourth season. The first season of *Cagney & Lacey* (1982) has been released on DVD and is also sometimes shown on classic television channels. So viewers are able to see Gless not only in her current role as Madeline Westin, the mother of Jeffrey Donovan's "burned" ex-spy character, but in her quintessential, Emmy-winning role of Christine Cagney. And now, they can discover yet another facet of Gless's extraordinary, versatile talent, as the witty, cantankerous, and moving character *Hannah Free*.

made a lot of creative decisions—whether it be casting, wardrobe, locations, camera movement or soundtrack—by trusting my gut, which was informed by my experience as a filmmaker for many years but also by close study of Claudia's great story.

JH: While you were directing, did you have some guiding principle or some goal as to how you wanted the film to be perceived?

WJC: It was important to me to portray Hannah and Rachel not just as young lovers but as older lovers as well, two women who share a deep emotional connection but also a passionate physical and sexual connection. And not to just imply that, but to show their attraction visually, cinematically. Most mainstream feature films don't show older couples sharing physical affection and sexual attraction for one another. Whether they are straight or queer, we just don't see many older characters in bed together or see older people kissing and being sensual together onscreen. I think it's sexy and fun and life affirming.

JH: Why do you think the relationship between these two women is so memorable?

WJC: Most long-term romantic relationships, regardless of orientation, wax and wane in the lust department. What's great about Hannah and Rachel is that theirs is the kind of great love affair that has sustained its passion and lust over decades, the kind of fantastic, enduring attraction and love that is celebrated and pined for in straight films all the time.

JH: If there is a political message embedded in the film, what do you think it is?

WJC: In addition to the story being about the letting go of someone we love, which we all experience at some point in life, I think the film really helps put a human face on the issue of equal

rights and human rights for every U.S. citizen. The Proposition 8 that passed in California is unjust and wrong. It makes me very sad and upset that we live in a culture where people are allowed to vote on who should remain second-class citizens. If we allow majority votes on civil and basic human rights, women and blacks still wouldn't have the right to vote.

JH: And what impact do you think the film will have, out in the world?

WJC: I hope the film continues to serve as a cultural force that can influence people, queer or straight, young or old, to do the right thing when the time comes, whether that means putting someone else's needs before your own or refusing to go along with the dehumanizing of others, especially others who are different from you. I think this film is very entertaining, sensual and provocative as a story of a great love affair. It's universal and will engage viewers regardless of sexual orientation. Hannah is a dynamic, sexy, flawed, passionate human being, and who can't relate to that? And Sharon Gless and the rest of the cast are such a pleasure to watch in every scene.

JH: Now that the film has premiered, do you have any further thoughts about its creation?

WJC: It was incredibly rewarding to work with such a great cast. The cast was the largest I've worked with in my career thus far, and they are all so talented and professional. So it pushed me as a director to not only have to decide what each scene meant to me at its core, but to also articulate that interpretation very clearly to the actors. I think being a good director also means listening to actors and working with them to create consistent emotional threads for their characters throughout the film.

On The Set
Hannah Free Stars Talk about the Film
by Jorjet Harper

Hannah Free, the new Chicago-produced film, is a lesbian love story spanning two women's lives. "Like so many good stories, *Hannah Free* is about people who forge a relationship without the benefit or burden of a roadmap," says Elaine Carlson, who plays the Day Nurse. "At a point in history where there isn't hope of anything resembling a traditional marriage, Rachel and Hannah form a bond that weathers the storms that come with age, conflicting interpretations of responsibility and difficult family members."

Jacqui Jackson, who stars as Greta, describes the main characters as "a pair of soul mates who love each other their whole lives. Hannah won't stay in one place, much as Rachel would like her to, and Rachel won't give herself over to publicizing her feelings, much as Hannah would like her to. We follow them as they grow from children to adults, and grow together as a couple, finding their medium and compromise. Until late in life, the two only need each other, but when Rachel falls into a coma, family jealousy keeps them apart."

As Carlson explains, "Hannah has spent a lifetime railing against restrictions, routines and schedules. How awful that age forces her into this small rectangle of a hospital bed! She has to endure the loss of her privacy, her independence, even control of her own bodily functions. The forced pleasantries of the nursing home staff infuriate her almost as much as the physical indignities. And as sympathetic as her caregivers are, when push comes to shove, schedules and regulations always seem to be the priority. The staff and volunteers at The Home—including my character, the Nurse—represent some of the last irritating obstacles that Hannah faces in her lifelong struggle to have things her own

way. But while she may lose a battle or two, Hannah does win the war."

Kelli Strickland plays Hannah as a young woman (Sharon Gless plays older Hannah). She agrees that the film is "a love story certainly, but that special kind of love story that spans decades and manages to survive the greatest of obstacles, including great distances, societal intolerance, and in many ways two very different world views—the kinds of obstacles that would have kept two people who were anything but soul mates apart."

Ongoing Connections

Hannah Free is based on a stage play by award-winning playwright Claudia Allen. Allen has been prominent in the Chicago theater community for many years and so was able to tap a lot of Chicago talent for the film. "I loved seeing how many people have gathered around Claudia, how she is a collector of people," says Taylor Miller, who plays Rachel's daughter Marge, the character who prevents Hannah from seeing her life partner in their old age. "I am a relatively new addition. Maybe five years have passed since I first met Claudia. I had done one of her plays, *Unspoken Prayers*—another lovely piece fraught with the human condition—at Victory Gardens Theater."

Some of the camaraderie on the set occurred because so many cast members had worked on Allen's plays before. Maureen Gallagher, who plays the Older Rachel in the film, had played Marge in 1996 at Victory Gardens—where Allen is a longtime Playwright in Residence—and had also taken Allen's playwriting classes. Elaine Carlson, playing the Nurse in the film, was Rachel in Bailiwick's stage production in 1992. "I'd met Claudia Allen earlier, when I went in as a replacement in the Chicago production of her *Gays of Our Lives*. That little romp proved to be just the beginning of an ongoing working relationship and a continuing friendship," recalls Carlson. Patricia Kane, who plays the Minister in the film, was also in the Victory Gardens production, playing multiple roles including the minister.

The film's Younger Hannah is played by Strickland, who had never acted in one of Allen's plays but had directed Allen's *Dutch Love* as part of the annual Pride Series at the Bailiwick. "(Producer) Tracy Baim called me the day before auditions and asked me to come in the next day and read. Initially, I thought she was asking me to come in and be a reader for the actors who were auditioning. I hadn't acted in a few years and was just happy to do what I thought was a favor for Claudia and Tracy. Little did I know that the favor was being bestowed upon me."

Strickland recalls her feeling at the first read-through with the cast: "looking around the table at all of the people who had been connected to Claudia's work over the years in so many ways. Laurie (Attea, the second assistant director, who had directed the original stage production of *Hannah Free*), Maureen, Pat, Elaine, Meg (Thalken), Les (Old Man), Sharon (Gless), Taylor and myself have either acted in or directed her plays over the last twenty years. It made me feel like a part of a legacy, and it made me supremely proud of Chicago theater."

Common Ground

Another shared experience for many of the cast members was a feeling that working on this film has changed them in some significant, positive way. Taylor Miller, who is probably best known for her long tenure on ABC's *All My Children*, reflects that she had never played a character who is not likeable before, yet "there is stuff in me that is just like Marge." Being able to understand the character sympathetically was useful to her to "not try to control those around me as a reason for how I act. It was not just this role that has sparked this, but a series of things that have been happening—kind of great that it is all changing me!"

Ann Hagemann, a straight actress who plays Rachel as a young woman, felt that she grew closer to her sister, who is a lesbian, during the filming. "I was able to draw on my experience with my sister. I'd leave the set and call my sister every night and

share my excitement about the film with her. She lives in a very conservative, smaller community that doesn't always embrace her lifestyle."

Being surrounded by a cast and crew that was largely lesbian and gay gave Hagemann a sense of the LGBT community she hadn't had before. It was, she says, "very enlightening to me. You can stand on the outside and say, 'oh, everybody's the same' but when you're actually in the inner circle and live and breathe and work daily with everyone, I felt like this light was around me all the time. And the beauty of this story is that we get to see the humanity of everybody. My character, Rachel, for much of her life, carried on this facade, and it wasn't till later in life that she embraced who she was. So it was cool for me to be among so many people who could be who they are."

Hagemann had not seen the play before auditioning but was familiar with Allen's work. "I knew the nature of the script. I went into this looking for a job, and came out of it knowing I'd had a life-altering experience."

Kelli Strickland was very aware, during the filming, of her character's place in time. "Hannah is a very specific character, but for me, as a lesbian, she also represents a generation of women to whom I am personally indebted for my freedom and the ease that I can walk through the world as an out lesbian. I felt an obligation to my community and to an audience to share my respect for her."

Social Relevance

Patricia Kane, who is also a lesbian, plays the self-righteous Minister whom Hannah encounters. Kane emphasizes the importance of the political connotations of the story. "These days, it's about having all our full rights. Access to your loved ones in hospice or medical care is a very prevalent issue for me and my partner, seeing the kind of hoops you have to go through." That aspect of the story has clarified the issue and thrown it into strong relief for Kane: "How love can be maintained despite obstacles

that are put on us by our family, our society and ourselves."

Kane also notes that there is a dearth of stories about lesbians in movies, especially about older lesbians. "I'm absolutely thrilled that Tracy, Sharon and Claudia were able to put this together. This is an important and ongoing story."

Jacqui Jackson, whose character Greta helps Hannah in her quest to be reunited with Rachel, sees Greta as "an advocate, and I really latched on to that idea. I am, like Greta, a queer woman who believes in human rights, and that helped fuel a lot of the scenes. Hannah's story is a perfect case of human rights denial: why should the life partner of a dying woman be denied access to see her in her final moments? I feel as strongly about the issue as Greta does in the script. The hardest part was the scene between Greta and Marge. It takes a lot of guts to stand up to a family member and tell them they're wrong. I hope that many people see it and are inspired to take steps toward putting some more understanding in the hearts of their friends and family."

Star Shines

The story of *Hannah Free* revolves around the title character, and Chicago cast members had many words of praise for the film's lead, television star Sharon Gless. Considering the reputation that many Hollywood stars have for being difficult, it was a pleasure for cast and crew to find Glass so genuine, warm and easy to work with.

"Sharon was a lovely, generous scene partner—one of the best," says Carlson. "I assumed we would approach our scenes as routine exposition. Goodness knows, Sharon had meatier scenes later in the story! Instead, I got to enjoy her full attention and creativity during those little opening scenes. I'm very grateful for that."

"It was great to work with Sharon, she was very open, very easy," agrees Gallagher, who, as the older Rachel, had some poignant scenes with Gless. "She had an understanding of the nuances of the scenes that I really appreciated."

For Kane, the entire shoot "was an absolute delight. Everyone was a delight, and working with Sharon was a blast. She's so easygoing, everything went so smoothly."

Strickland, as the younger version of Gless's character, had no scenes with Gless, "but my first meeting with her was one of the most memorable of the entire process. At our first rehearsal, the adult Hannahs and adult Rachels met. Sharon had laryngitis and had absolutely no voice. She came into the room that would eventually be transformed into Hannah and Rachel's living room, took my face in her hands, looked into my eyes and whispered 'I see me in you.' The generosity and intensity with which she met me gave me goose bumps. But while all of that was going on, there was this small voice in the back of my head thinking 'Cagney is smooshing my face!!!'"

Keeping it Real

Strickland also had much praise for the film's director, Wendy Jo Carlton. "To be honest, I was incredibly nervous at first. Wendy Jo was great about keeping things specific. Before we began filming, Wendy Jo called me just to say hello and ask me if I had any questions. I think I unleashed on her this torrent of anxiety. Just expressing all of that nervousness seemed to be enough to calm those fears and Wendy Jo, in her very unflappable, calm way, was able to remind me that we are just storytellers, telling this one specific story. Once I got back to that, it was a joy!"

Strickland had some lingering concerns about her character's sex scenes. "Does it need to be said that all of the sex scenes were nerve-wracking?? The scenes with Rachel and Hannah earlier in their lives are the manifestation of that magnetic pull, the intense physical attraction, the emotional intimacy that Hannah shares with no one but Rachel. But once again, Wendy Jo created an environment that was so supportive and calm. She and the crew were remarkably kind and respectful."

Gallagher had similar praise for the positive tone on the set in general. "As an actor, I thought it was a delightful experience,

a great shoot, because being in that house (the South Side Chicago home where the interior scenes were filmed) was so cool. Just to go there every day was so unique, and to have us all in there together, the cast and crew, was a very supportive, happy atmosphere all around."

Miller says she feels fortunate "to be part of a project as important as this one—one that shows so clearly the love these women had for each other, putting a human face on the gay-rights issue."

"The main message is the power of love," reflects Hagemann. "Love is not judgmental; it's not always kind, but you cannot deny it when it's there, and *Hannah Free* reveals the true humanity in all of us."

"Wendy Jo, Tracy and the entire production crew were warm and professional," adds Carlson. "I'll hold fond memories of the *Hannah Free* shoot for a long, long time."

Jorjet Harper was an extra in *Hannah Free*, and some of her paintings can be seen in the film.

Sharon Gless—*Hannah Free* Q&A
For Windy City Times
September 16, 2009
by Richard Knight, Jr.

When actress Sharon Gless and I first talked in November of 2008 she had just finished a long day shooting her first movie in years. Taking a break from her nearly constant TV work— she was at that time finishing up her character arc on *Nip/Tuck*, contemplating a second season on *Burn Notice*, reminiscing about her beloved Debbie Novotny character on *Queer As Folk* (which put Showtime on the map) and her breakout role in *Cagney & Lacey*—Gless was nothing if not a whirlwind of energy. The long day's shoot hadn't dimmed her enthusiasm for her first starring film role—playing the feisty lesbian in the film adaptation of Claudia Allen's acclaimed stage play *Hannah Free*, or her desire to talk about it.

Now, almost a year after our initial conversation, the work completed, *Hannah Free* has triumphed as it has played the film festival circuit (it was honored with the closing night of the Frameline festival where it was introduced by Rosie O'Donnell). What follows are excerpts from our conversation, conducted in my role as cinema reviewer of Windy City Times in Chicago.

WINDY CITY TIMES (WCT): I don't know much about *Hannah Free* other than it's based on Claudia Allen's 1991 stage play and that it's about a lesbian couple. Can you tell me a little bit more about it?

SHARON GLESS (SG): That's it! (laughs)

WCT: Their life together?

SG: Yes, it's about their life together…and apart. They've fallen in love when they were very, very young—as children. In fact, we're portrayed by three different generations. Rachel, the one who is the object of Hannah's affections, is not out. In fact, she wishes that there were no Hannah. It's not a life that she wanted but she couldn't help it. She loved her. But Hannah pursues her through all her life; loves her; they love each other. And they do have sex eventually. Rachel is stuck in her world and her town and cannot be out and she marries—she says to get away from her father—has children and does the right things, you know? Whereas Hannah is much more comfortable in her own body— she knows who she is, she doesn't make any bones about it. So Rachel marries and Hannah leaves town but in Rachel's defense, Hannah would have left town anyway. Hannah travels all over the world; she's very independent, randy, has other women in other towns.

WCT: A free spirit.

SG: Yes. But she always returns for Rachel. The thrust of the story takes place in a nursing home where they're now in their late 70s, 80s. Hannah's still very strong-willed; has to rule from a bed in a nursing home. In the same nursing home is Rachel who had a stroke and has been in a coma for nine months or so. The conflict in the present day story is that Hannah is trying to get to the wing of this nursing home in another building where Rachel is dying and her daughter will not allow Hannah inside the room.

WCT: Ooh.

SG: And Hannah helped raise this kid but she will not sit for disturbing her mother. Rachel's in a coma. Hannah is very frightened that Rachel will die alone and all Hannah asks is to say goodbye.

WCT: It's like one of those petty things that great tragedies hinge on—like the lead character in *A Trip to Bountiful* just wanting to go home one last time before she dies and the daughter-in-law blocking her. It sounds tremendously moving.

SG: Yes—but there's always humor going on within this sadness. She has that gift—Claudia does—to just take pathos and all of a sudden you're laughing within the most tragic situations. It's a great story. It's funny, it's sad. You see the children adorable in overalls saying, "Kiss me, okay now it's your turn to kiss me"— you know, like children do?

WCT: What a great part for you.

SG: Ooh—it's a wonderful part.

WCT: Now, am I right—this is your feature film debut?

SG: Well, it isn't actually. I did one when I was a contract player at Universal. All of us were stewardesses in *Airport '75*. We didn't have any dialogue but we were paid anyway.

WCT: (imitating Karen Black) "I can't fly the plane!"

SG: (laughing) At least I was in first class! I didn't get to talk but at least I was in first class. Then I did a movie with Michael Douglas in *The Star Chamber* and I played his wife. It was one of his least successful films but anyway, I did do it. And with this—and it is Screen Actor's Guild—I could become a member of the Motion Picture Academy because it's my third one. (laughs hard)

WCT: The perks! That's delightful. Then you can get—

SG: —all those movie screeners! My husband's a member and gets them but I want my own. He never lets me show them to anybody.

WCT: How did the material come to you? Did they send it to your agent?

SG: No, Claudia Allen just called me. I was here (in Chicago) to get an award from DePaul University—they honored me this year, their theatre section—and I called Claudia and said, "I'm in town, come and have dinner with me" and she mentioned it then and then she called me and said, "I'm serious. We're really going to make this into a film" so we had to make the time work out and everything so here I am.

WCT: Your *Burn Notice* character is another great, complicated character like Colleen Rose who you played on *Nip/Tuck*.

SG: Colleen Rose!

WCT: I love Ryan Murphy (creator/writer of *Nip/Tuck*)—he's so twisted.

SG: He did tailor it for me. He says it's the sickest he's ever done (laughs). Have you seen it?

WCT: Oh yes.

SG: (Does Colleen) "It's the best bear I ever made."

WCT: Now of course, we have to talk about Debbie Novotny, your wonderful character from *Queer As Folk*.

SG: I was here, you know, when I got that script. It was sneaked to me. I was doing Claudia's play *Cahoots* and I asked for the finest drama coach in the city of Chicago to help me do Eleanor of Aquitaine for *A Lion in Winter* later—I was going to go on and do that after *Cahoots*. So they called Peter Forrester who was fabulous. At night he was a drama coach and during

the day he was an actor's agent and he had a copy of this script called *Queer As Folk* and he sneaked it to me. I read it and I called Showtime and I said, "Is this role cast?" and they said, "Nothing's cast yet" and I said, "I want it." And because of him I did *Queer As Folk* for five years and it changed my life. It changed my life, my career, everything.

WCT: Can you imagine how Debbie Novotny would be with this Proposition 8 bullshit? She'd be on the front lines.

SG: Oh yeah. We did an episode about my son getting married. They bicycle to Toronto from Pittsburgh and while they're up there Michael and (the character Bobby Gant played) get married and when they come back through they can't get in the country and Debbie was engaged to be married and I had that wonderful speech where I said, "I will not walk down the aisle until my son is also allowed to walk down the aisle."

WCT: Seems like we've come a long way but...

SG: ...but we haven't. Well, we have our first African-American president but we're still the most homophobic country in the world. It'll change. It can't stay. It's unconstitutional.

WCT: When you took the part of Debbie, even as late as 2000, I remember it was a little controversial. I remember how down and dirty it was and some of the coverage had the tone of, "Sharon Gless is on this really out-there show" and I'm guessing you got a little bit of flak for that; did you?

SG: Nobody ever gave me any trouble. I signed on because I love trouble—I wanted trouble (laughs). I couldn't wait for the night we premiered because I figured the Religious Right would go bonkers and unfortunately we premiered while the Republicans were literally stealing the presidency in Florida. It was that night—you remember when they were fixing the

machines. I mean they rigged it. Let's face it, Gore was president. So the Religious Right was busy trying to get their idiot in so nobody noticed. We just sort of slipped in and we missed all the trouble I thought we'd get (laughs).

WCT: It's so great to see you go from a part like Debbie Novotny to *Nip/Tuck* to *Burn Notice* and now Hannah. They all seem to be very complicated women—where do you draw from as an actor? Do you have a process? How do you get to that emotional place?

SG: I don't know how I do it. I don't know how I'm going to do it (Hannah's last scene). I'm afraid of that scene. I haven't thought about it yet. I'll probably play a tune in my head—something that we danced to when we were young in our living room because we couldn't do it in public or she wouldn't do it in public.

WCT: I know that Jessica Lange uses different smells to help her. In Streetcar she had a perfumed hanky that would take her to an emotional place.

SG: Oh wow. No, no, I have no method. I'm not like that. I just believe I'm that person with all my heart and for a space of time I'm...Hannah and I have to love this person enough to do it. Emotional recall doesn't always work. You know, you think about your grandmother dying—some days it makes you cry, some days it doesn't. You can't depend on it so I just really believe that I'm Hannah and I believe I love this woman. I'm taking the woman out who's playing the coma Rachel for dinner Saturday night. We're going to have a date.

WCT: (laughs) That's so great.

SG: I know. I just thought we should get to know one another. I have some kissing scenes with her next week in the barn.

WCT: Wonderful. I love that. I want to come back for the kissing scenes.

SG: Well, it's not all that. It's the 30 year-olds who get nude and get it on. Who wants to see this compared to that (laughs)? But still, I'm going to kiss her on the mouth.

WCT: Good for you.

SG: Oh yeah! I'm *Hannah Free*.

WCT: Now, unfortunately the lesbian-themed films haven't had as much success in recent years as the gay ones. *The Advocate* did a piece recently about how hard it is to get the lesbian ladies to go out and see these movies.

SG: It shouldn't be made just for the gays and the lesbians. It should be made, like *Brokeback Mountain*, for everybody. But now I'm contradicting myself because *Queer As Folk* was made just for the gay audience. Made by gay producers, made for the gay audience, they didn't try to pull any punches; they didn't try to please everybody. But everybody started watching; fifty percent more audience signed on than they planned and there were a lot of straight women because they wanted to watch these guys get it on—hello! And they'd watch with their boyfriends and the girls would get hot looking at the guys do it and the boyfriends would get laid that night. It all worked out very nicely (laughs hard). Why are you surprised? There's not a straight man in the world—whether they admit it or not—who wouldn't love to watch two women going at it. It's every man's fantasy so why shouldn't the women enjoy watching the guys?

WCT: We haven't even touched on your first and perhaps most memorable television success, *Cagney and Lacy*. Are you in touch with Tyne Daly, your co-star?

SG: Yes, we're very close friends. Her mom had a great expression—"Sweat is a great cement" and we sweated together for six years, Tyne Daly and I did against all odds, against the world sometimes. By the time we were over we'd been thrown off the air three times, some of our shows were banned by certain affiliates—too controversial. But while we were on the air no other actress ever won the Emmy.

WCT: That's quite a tribute right there.

SG: Yes it is. Tyne won the first three, I won the next two and we thought we'd tie but it went back to her.

WCT: So where does this spicy maverick streak come from?

SG: You mean in me?

WCT: Yes—because it's all through your career.

SG: I don't know. I think I just came in this way. If you asked for a description of what I was like as a little girl, I was a good little girl—sweet and well behaved. My parents were very strict but I think there always was, I don't know, I guess, that thing in me.

WCT: You're like a real-life Hannah Free.

SG: Yeah!

WCT: Straight version.

SG: (laughs) Yeah! No, I don't know if I'm as brave as Hannah. Hannah was very brave, the things she did. I wasn't as brave as Hannah, though I do consider myself brave every time I go in front of the camera. I think that's an act of courage. Especially

WCT: My acting friends tell me that the most intense movies often have the liveliest sets—to relieve the tension—have you found that to be true?

SG: Well I like quiet around me when I'm working but once those intense scenes are over, yes—let's party—I'm so glad that's over (laughs). But, overall, I'm just very grateful that they're still letting me do it. Most actresses my age aren't working. All the big motion picture stars my age can't get arrested—except Meryl Streep. Television is now where it's at. Now of course, television is turning its back on its Emmy-winning actresses and taking in movie stars. But listen, they're wonderful and they're writing some nice things for women again now. So that's why I come from gratitude every day because so far they still let me in.

WCT: I think I speak for a lot of people when I say that it's great to have you "in."

SG: (laughs) Thank you so much for that. I'm loving this movie and this part. It's a real labor of love. This is Mickey and Judy in the barn doing a show. I don't know what's going to happen with it but I feel it's going to be seen. I certainly hope so because it's worthy—really worthy.

From Stage to Film
Laurie Attea on the set of *Hannah Free*
by Jorjet Harper

In some way, Laurie Attea set everything in motion. She discovered Claudia Allen's play *Hannah Free* in a pile at the Bailiwick Repertory theater and decided to direct it. This original stage production of *Hannah Free* was produced in 1992. When the play was about to be filmed, in 2008, Attea was asked to help with the casting. "I then got swept up in the idea of the production," she says, and she became not only Casting Director for the film but also 2nd Assistant Director, a job she had never done before.

She was a fast learner. During filming, Attea was a ubiquitous presence, clipboard in hand. "As it turns out, the job of the 2nd AD is very similar to that of a stage manager on stage," she says. "You're the first one on set and the last to leave. There's lots of paperwork. But one of my primary roles was acting as liaison between the actors and the set, which I very much enjoyed. I also organized the extras, dealt with call times for cast and crew and tried to keep things running on schedule."

Looking back on the original play, staged at Bailiwick, Attea says, "I'm not sure that the message has changed any from when we first produced the play. We didn't have a lot of media role models back then, the movies and television shows didn't have gay and lesbian characters as a matter of course. I think it is much easier now for people to hear and respond to some of the issues because they are more in the forefront of our thinking and more possible now. I think it was also harder to be in a gay or lesbian relationship twenty-five years ago than it is now. We now have many examples of lesbian couples in long-term relationships. I can offer mine as being one: my partner Lauren and I have been together nineteen years."

Not only was it more difficult to be accepted as a same-sex couple years ago, but "the negative connotations made it difficult for some gays or lesbians to accept themselves. Of course, the small-town aspect is still alive—it is still not easy being gay or lesbian in a small town." With the advent of gay marriage and domestic-partner rights (in some states), says Attea, "we've come a long way in some aspects and in some areas. Being able to care for the person you love should be a right for any person regardless of sexual orientation. I think *Hannah Free* reminds us of that as we continue with that struggle now."

Attea explained some of the practical differences between the staging of the play and the shooting of the film. "One of the differences between the script and screenplay is the amount of roles. In the stage play, the actresses playing Hannah and Rachel played them at all ages," while in the film, different actresses of different ages were needed to show the two main characters at different stages in their lives. Also, "the stage play didn't have as many sex scenes (or any at all, I think). It was a more innocent play; we saw the characters' deep love for each other, but not so much the sexual passion."

Among the group of actors who worked on the film, Attea points out that many had been in previous stage productions of *Hannah Free*. "I don't think any of them, except Pat Kane, played the same roles, but it is a testament to Claudia Allen and this play that so many of them wanted to be a part of the film. A woman who had played the role of Hannah in a Madison production, Sarah Newport, even drove to Chicago from Madison, just to be an extra in the film!"

Since the interior scenes were shot in a historic 19th century South Side mansion, creaking floors and other noises needed to be silenced during the shooting so as not to spoil the scenes, and this too was part of Attea's job. "We had PAs (production assistants) stationed throughout the house, at the back door, upstairs and sometimes even outside to try and keep everyone quiet when we were shooting." PAs communicated with each other by headsets so they would know when they needed to keep

everyone quiet. PAs shouted "Lock it up!" whenever the cameras began rolling. The squeaking floors were a problem because, Attea explains, "any movement could be picked up by the audio techs, so we needed to keep people quiet near the set, outside the set and above the set. We were all in very close quarters on these sets, so any unwanted sound could ruin a take. At times, a lot of people had to fit into small spaces to shoot the scenes."

There was also the problem of noises from the urban environment. "Many times there would be outside noise that we had to go out and try and stop. Trucks or kids playing, lawns being mowed, etc. Not everyone wanted to stop what they were doing because we were shooting a movie, but I think most people tried to accommodate us." When the crew was short handed, entry doors would be locked so no one would burst in, making noise, in the middle of a take. Even with the closed doors, heat was difficult to maintain in the huge, rambling house. "I remember it was always very cold in the house and people were usually in their coats, hats, scarves etc. I always had multiple layers on to keep myself warm."

Attea says it was "a great learning experience, and a pleasure for me. I appreciate and respect actors a great deal, and I had a wonderful group of actors and extras that I worked with on this film."

Sharon Zurek
Hannah Free Editor Extraordinaire
by Jorjet Harper

Hannah Free, the story of a lifelong lesbian relationship, was filmed in Chicago in 2008. It was finished just in time for a gala San Francisco premiere in June 2009, thanks to the efforts of editor Sharon Zurek.

Zurek, owner of Black Cat Productions in Chicago, has worked on many independent features, short films and social issue documentaries. Her GLBT projects prior to *Hannah Free* include directing *Kevin's Room* and working on Catherine Crouch's lesbian-themed *Stray Dogs*, starring actress Guinevere Turner of *Go Fish*. Zurek has also worked on mainstream projects, including producing, directing and editing commercials. She edited the detective drama *Dirty Work*, which was shot in Chicago; the 2005 film *The Trouble with Dee Dee*, directed by Mike Meiners; and recently she was post-production supervisor on Michael Keaton's *The Merry Gentleman* (2008).

Zurek was in the midst of editing two documentary films when she was contacted about Hannah Free. "It sounded exciting, but I wasn't sure I could do it because I had other projects, so the timing almost didn't work." Fortunately, Zurek's other clients "were kind enough to let me put them on hold a little bit to work on *Hannah Free*. That's one of the nice things about independent filmmakers, everybody tries to work things out."

Zurek, a lesbian, was impressed by the project. "When you see the script," says Zurek, "the words just feel very familiar and natural. I really do think Claudia Allen's story and dialogue are terrific." And, she adds, "What lesbian wouldn't want to be editing Sharon Gless? It was a pure pleasure to be working with her performance. I would have to say that the performances in *Hannah Free* were very enjoyable to work with. Often it wasn't

looking for the Moment of a scene but choosing between two or more equally good scenes that drove the story in the direction it had to go."

Generally in any movie, Zurek explains, the story is told at least three times: "when you write it, when you shoot it, and when you edit it. Because what you have on paper is not always what you get when you shoot it, and what you end up with in the edit room is pretty much your story, your final result. Filmmakers are sometimes afraid of that process, though some with more experience end up embracing it, once they understand the power you have in the edit room to make things work. I've done production and it's exhausting. In the edit room, you see that Moment. I love that. When you edit, you are working with what you have to work with, finding the best moments and pieces to make your movie."

Independent films don't usually have the luxury of doing an editor's cut, a director's cut and a producer's cut, however, and this was certainly true of *Hannah Free*. "We pretty much started with a first assembly, and then (*Hannah Free* Director) Wendy Jo [Carlton] came in. As an editor, you try to get into the head of the director as quickly as possible, so I always consider it a success when I can anticipate what the director wants to have happen next, before they even speak. I think of myself as a facilitator. It's not my movie. I want to help them tell their story and hopefully bring some great ideas in."

There was a short window of time to edit the film, after a short three-week shoot in November, 2008; during the shoot Zurek's assistant Justine Gendron worked assembling scenes. At the same time, Sarah Plano worked as data wrangler, a necessary assistant on the set when shooting digitally rather than on film. "We worked on the trailer in December and started mid-January to produce an assembly edit," says Zurek. A rough cut was sent to Frameline, the San Francisco GLBT film festival, in March in order to qualify for the 2009 festival. "That's a pretty risky thing to do, but we had a great story and great performances," says Zurek. The festival staff must have agreed, because not only did they

approve the film based on the rough cut, but also programmed the film for Closing Night, a coveted spot in the lineup. The final cut was ready in time for the June 28 premiere, on the evening of Pride Sunday in San Francisco. Sharon Gless made a personal appearance, and the film was introduced by Gless's friend Rosie O'Donnell, whom Gless had met when O'Donnell appeared in several episodes of *Queer As Folk*.

Editing *Hannah Free* had a close personal meaning for Zurek as well. "Being a lesbian, having been in a relationship with a woman for twenty years, and having lost her to cancer, it was pretty close. It gives us the validity that our lives matter, that we actually exist, and that there are many of us who go through this. So my biggest regret, of course, was that my partner wasn't here to see this movie. She would have been so thrilled to see it and be around during the creation of it. I know she would have enjoyed it as much as we did."

The grueling schedule was, nevertheless, a challenge for Zurek, music and sound director Martie Marro, and director Wendy Jo Carlton. "We laughed, we cried, we didn't sleep much. I think our biorhythms could keep each other out of despair. The friendships go deep, because it's very emotionally intense spending sixty to eighty hours a week with somebody over a period of months. When we're old and gray and bump into each other in the future, we'll just have to look at each other and there will be an immediate shorthand."

Zurek also credits producer Tracy Baim for her role in realizing *Hannah Free*. "This was her first time producing a movie, and she chose to allow us to do what we were experienced doing, and tried to stay out of the way, and as she learned what she needed to be doing, she was there, a quick study, asking questions. She's a great reporter, so she gets the facts and then she runs with them." Despite the pressure of such a short time frame to finish *Hannah Free*, Zurek is pleased to have been the film's editor. "Every person involved was vital in some way to the making of this film, and that doesn't always happen. It was a blessing, so you go with it."

Perfect Pitch
Hannah Free Composer Martie Marro
by Jorjet Harper

As music and sound director for the independent film *Hannah Free*, Martie Marro had a great deal of responsibility for the emotional depth of the film's story. In addition to providing the emotional glue holding the film together, she had to deal with the difficulties of a clean soundtrack in a shooting venue often marred by the extraneous sounds of the urban environment.

Luckily, Marro is a technological wizard and something of a Renaissance woman. She is founder and owner of Materville Studios, a state-of-the-art multi media recording lab that was designed to handle projects for film, video, digital animation, paints, fashion, photography, printed media, radio and music, and combinations of these media.

She also runs Love Your Website, a web hosting service providing Web design, maintenance, and many other Web services for its customers. Through Love Your Website, Marro is able to incorporate all of Materville's projects into highly technical multimedia Web sites. These have included rich databases of Chicago literature, music, news and history.

Marro is also a member of band Stewed Tomatoes, the "all-female indie pop punk sex funk rock phenomenon" that has appeared in many Chicago venues and in other cities throughout the Midwest. And she has a decade of FM radio production experience, doing commercials, interviews and musical backbeds.

As a woman who has successfully combined business and artistic pursuits, Marro has received many awards for her work, including the Windy City Times and IBM excellence award, a Gay and Lesbian Music Award nomination for Best Video, and an OUT Music nomination for Musician of the Year. Her work on *Hannah Free* won the film two OutMusic Awards at the end

of 2009. Marro can be heard on many soundtracks, including Francis Ford Coppola's *First Wave* television series. She topped the charts at No. 1 on the world charting system for MP3.com. And she has been dubbed "Download Babe of the Day" by Tech TV's *Internet Tonight*.

Marro has created sound and music for *Dance Floor Battle Scars, The Gendercator, Buttery Top, Maybe, Coup d'etat,* Canadian short *Tunnel Vision* and *Gayco Expose,* a comedy. Beginning her long career in post-production, Martie worked on sound repair of many more films, enjoying the challenge of removing the sound of locusts, trains, rumbling trucks and accidental crew noises.

In short, Marro was a perfect choice to supervise sound and compose the score for *Hannah Free,* the premiere film from Ripe Fruit Films, founded in 2008 "to produce Chicago-based films about lesbian lives."

Both the film shoot and post production on *Hannah Free* were on a super tight schedule. "We wanted to get music involved as soon as possible," says Sharon Zurek, *Hannah Free's* editor and one of the executive producers of the film. "The sooner the composer can think about scenes or how different instruments might speak to different characters, the better." Once the editing phase began in January, Marro spent an enormous, concentrated amount of time working on the film with Zurek and director Wendy Jo Carlton. "We were joined at the hips for several months," quips Zurek. This dedication paid off, as the film was able to debut in June at a gala event in San Francisco.

After immersing herself in every aspect of the sound of *Hannah Free,* Marro finds that odd bits still stick in her mind. "In the ensuing months since production on *Hannah Free,* I have often caught myself repeating lines of the movie in regular conversation," says Marro. "On this most recent Mother's Day, for instance, my mom was complaining of minor aches and pains all over her body, and out my mouth popped: "You are just refining yourself down to the essentials, right?" This is one of Hannah's more philosophical reflections in the film.

Marro also enjoyed working with star Sharon Gless. "My favorite line of the whole movie is when Hannah (played by Gless) says, 'Get a grip on yourself.' She has the cutest smile on her face, with the sparkle of a five-year-old darling."

HANNAH FREE

The following is an abbreviated list of credits for the film version of Hannah Free, by Ripe Fruit Films. See www.hannahfree.com, or the film itself, for complete credits list and information on the film.

Hannah (1970s-1990s)	Sharon Gless
Rachel (1970s-1990s)	Maureen Gallagher
Hannah (1930s-1940s)	Kelli Strickland
Rachel (1930s-1940s)	Ann Hagemann
Hannah (1920s)	Casey Tutton
Rachel (1920s)	Elita Ernsteen
Marge	Taylor Miller
Greta	Jacqui Kate Jackson
Mail Lady	Meg Thalken
Day Nurse	Elaine Carlson
Minister	Patricia Kane
Old Man	Les Hinderyckx
Night Nurse	Bev Spangler
Male Nurse	Brad Harbaugh
Woman in Bar	Kate D. Mahoney
Activities Nurse	Shawn Murray
Old Man with Walker	Dennis Stewart
Director	Wendy Jo Carlton
Screenwriter	Claudia Allen
Produced by	Tracy Baim, Sharon Zurek, Martie Marro, Wendy Jo Carlton
Director of Photography	Gretchen Warthen
Editor	Sharon Zurek
Music Composer	Martie Marro
Production Designer	Rick Paul
Costume Designer	Iris Bainum-Houle
Casting Director	L.M. Attea